Forty Hours

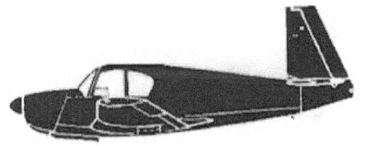

by

Mike Farris

Cover design: Chris Holmes

Paranormalice Press, LLC
Ormond Beach, FL 32174
www.paranormalice.com
paranormalicepress@gmail.com
Cover Art by Chris Holmes
Produced in the U.S.A

In memory of my parents, Corky and Juanita Farris

Acknowledgments

This year marks the fifty-seventh anniversary of my father's plane crash in a heavily forested area of southeast Texas known as the Big Thicket. I was nine years old at the time, but even then I realized how significant this was in my life and that of my entire family. I have always believed it to be a story worth telling.

I made the decision this year to finally do exactly that. Rather than a strict, non-fiction account, however, I opted to novelize portions of it, not to sensationalize the event but to serve the telling of the story. In particular, I hit upon the idea of having the pilot who was killed in the crash appear as some sort of apparition—it's an open question whether he is an angel, a ghost, or a hallucination—in order to engage in dialogue with my dad during his forty hours on the floor of the Big Thicket.

Relying upon a transcript of an account my dad gave, in detail, of the events of those forty hours, as well as other papers and sermons of his, I created that back-and-forth between him and the pilot.

Thanks, as usual, to my agent Donna Eastman, who continues to believe in my work. Thanks, too, to the team at Paranormalice for believing in this book, including executive editor Veronica H. Hart and editor Marie McIntyre.

I also must thank my brother, Steve Farris, and sister, Darlyne Farris Jackson, who shared this experience in our lives and encouraged me to write about it. Sadly, Darlyne passed away earlier this year and never saw the final product.

Of course, continued thanks to my wife Susan for her unceasing love and support.

Finally, I have to acknowledge and thank my parents, Dr. T.V. "Corky" and Juanita Farris, both of whom have passed away, for being the inspirational influences in my life that I hope are reflected in the characters in this book.

Forty Hours

CHAPTER ONE

Tuesday, January 12, 1965

I saw nothing but blackness, felt nothing but a dull ache in my head. A tingling, almost electric sensation traversed my lower back. No sensation at all in either leg. A tightness gripped my chest, squeezing the breath from my diaphragm. Panic gained a solid toehold as I tried to put together the sequence of events that had brought me here, but my memory was hazy.

I remembered getting in on the passenger side of a Mooney Mark 21 single engine aircraft, a green and white four-seater owned and piloted by my friend Gabriel Rogers, on a rudimentary airstrip surrounded by towering trees. That was around 10:00 p.m. on Tuesday. A few hours earlier, we had arrived at that same airstrip, which was owned by Texas Pulp and Paper Company on the outskirts of the tiny east Texas town of Evadale in Jasper County.

Located about twenty-five miles northeast of the coastal town of Beaumont, with its economy again vitalized by the pulp and paper industry, Evadale's population had surged into the 700s after falling to below 100 following the closing of the Kirby Mill during the Depression and aftereffects of World War II's drain of manpower and jobs.

As an associate with the Baptist General Convention of Texas, I had accepted an invitation from the pastor of a Baptist church in the town of Kountze, about seventeen miles west of Evadale. I spoke at a clinic for pastors of churches making up the Southeast Texas Baptist Association in anticipation of their participation in an upcoming Evangelism Conference to be held in Dallas beginning on January 18th. I also had made a similar presentation in the Texas panhandle on Monday, the day before, diagonally across the state. Gabe, whom I had known for a few years and who lived with his wife just down the street from my family in the Dallas suburb of Duncanville, had volunteered to fly me to both locations. That way, I wouldn't have to spend hours on the road or incur the expense of flying commercially, followed by car rentals.

The evening session was conducted at a church in Evadale, host for the meeting, where its pastor introduced me to the group as Dr. Corky Farris, rather than by my more formal name of Theron V. Farris, which I have always hated. The pastor briefly touched on my position with the BGCT and noted that I had, prior to that, served five years as a missionary to Japan. All of that, I supposed, was to lend credibility to whatever I might say about evangelism.

I could barely remember any specifics about the meeting, itself. Sometimes those things all blended together, but I did recall that after the meeting, Gabe and I debated whether to fly home the next morning, as originally planned, or to depart Tuesday night. The former presented some logistical problems. Even at 700 souls and a booming pulp and paper economy, the closest motel to Evadale was a number of miles away. One of our hosts had graciously invited us to spend the night at his family's home, but we hated to inconvenience him.

Besides, when Gabe contacted the weather bureau at Mid-County Airport in nearby Beaumont to inquire about weather conditions, he was advised of a heavy, and low, cloud ceiling expected in the morning, hovering at roughly 800 feet above sea level. Although that might seem high enough, our flight path, at least initially as we took off from an airstrip surrounded by thick woods, would carry us over the treetops of an 80,000-plus acre swath of southeast Texas's Piney Woods known as the Big Thicket. Trees in the Thicket could easily top out at over 150 feet. Couple that with an upslope in ground elevation as we moved farther inland from the Texas Gulf coast, ultimately rising another couple of hundred feet, and a fog ceiling at 800 feet could present a real problem.

Maneuvering through low clouds in order to maintain altitude above the trees, even if just long enough to circumnavigate the Thicket, would be tricky for Gabe, who was not instrument-rated and would have to rely on visual flight rules. Avoiding treetops as ground elevation rose could well force the small aircraft right into the thick of that expected soup.

But the ceiling was more than sufficiently high that night in southeast Texas, 13,000 feet according to the Beaumont station, and even higher at Redbird Airport, Gabe's home base just south of Dallas. So, rather than impose on the hospitality of our host for that spare bedroom, Gabe and I decided it made more sense to return to Dallas that night. And, after spending the prior night in the Texas panhandle, I was anxious to get home to Juanita and the kids. I didn't figure any of them would object to my early return, even if late at night.

Gabe, with his strong chin and well-groomed hair, clad in a brown leather flight jacket, fit the "central casting" stereotype for a pilot. His very appearance inspired confidence in his flying skills. On the other hand, I hoped I didn't fit the stereotype for an evangelist, given that those were so often negative. I wore my black hair stylishly long, though it was starting ever so slightly to turn gray at the temples. My most prominent feature was likely a nose that bent noticeably, having been broken two times already in my short thirty-seven years of existence.

Gabe got in on the pilot's side, and we both buckled up. He started the engine and taxied to the end of the runway, where he spun around and began his acceleration to take-off. It seemed to me that it took forever to achieve the appropriate speed, but finally we lifted off. Once we got airborne, Gabe circled the airstrip and waggled his wings, cue to the ground crew – which consisted solely of the church member who drove us to our plane from the meeting – to kill the airstrip's lights and go home. After Gabe attained his desired elevation above the surrounding treetops, he leveled off and headed toward Dallas.

Our path would take us northwest, skirting the town of Woodville and then on to Dallas, about 280 miles from Evadale. Below us, I could just make out a darkness that I knew was the heavily-wooded part of east Texas known simply, and descriptively, as the Big Thicket. With its swamps, rivers, and dense forest, as well as critters ranging from alligators and snakes to panthers and bobcats, the Big Thicket's lore was replete with stories of people who went in and never came out.

As a native Texan, born and raised in Fort Worth, I had long heard of the Big Thicket and the myths surrounding it. Like the Light of Saratoga, sometimes called the Bragg Road Ghost Light, a mysterious light that randomly appeared and disappeared in the night. Legend had it that it was wielded by the ghost of a railroad worker who had been decapitated on the railroad tracks that once transected the woods, while he searched for his missing head. There was even some talk of a Bigfoot creature, though no sightings had ever been corroborated. All reason enough, though, to never set foot in there after dark. Or maybe not even in daylight, for that matter.

"I've got a question for you," Gabe said, after we levelled off.

"Fire away."

"I feel like I've gotten to know you a little bit these past few years, but I've only heard you preach a few times. When we first met, I figured you were one of those Bible-thumpers, but now I'm starting to think you're one of the cerebral types."

I smiled. The reputations of countless hellfire-and-brimstone Baptist preachers preceded me, but they needn't define me. "I'd like to think I'm a little of both," I answered.

"And I'd like to think I'm part Charles Lindbergh and part Chuck Yeager."

"At least you didn't say Wiley Post and Amelia Earhart."

"Who's Wiley Post?"

"He's the guy who flew the plane that crashed with Will Rogers on board."

"Funny stuff," Gabe said. But his tone belied what he said. I figured he didn't take plane crashes lightly. That attitude was fine by me.

"Sorry, I didn't mean anything by it."

"I know. No harm, no foul. But getting back to my point. You believe in God, right? I mean, we both do, right?"

"It's pretty much my number one job requirement."

This time he smiled. Then he took a deep breath. "So, here's my question. If there really is a God, and if God is good and great and perfect, then why is there so much bad in the world?"

And there it was: the question that went right to the heart of the matter. I'd heard it asked dozens of times before, in all sorts of ways and coming from every possible angle. If God is perfect, why are people imperfect? If God is love, why is there hate? If God is righteous, why is there evil? Why is there pain and sorrow and heartache? Why doesn't God intervene and right all the wrongs and heal all the brokenness? If God is sitting on His throne in heaven, and if He loves all of us, why does He send men and women and children to hell? He could just snap his fingers and fix it all, just like that. How can you believe in a God who allows the bad when He has the power to ensure the good?

"Because there's also a Satan," I said. "And a little something called free will."

"What's that got to do with anything?"

"God didn't just make a bunch of robots. He also gave us free will, to choose for ourselves what to believe and what to do. Way back there in the Garden of Eden, God gave Adam and Eve a choice. They just made the wrong one, and that choice brought evil into an otherwise perfect world. But that wasn't God's fault. Choices have consequences."

As if on cue with the word "consequences," our tiny plane flew into a patch of thick clouds, obscuring vision through the front windshield.

Gabe adjusted the plane's elevation and dipped below the cloud cover. "That's lower than they told us."

"By how much?"

"I'd say hundreds of feet. If we hit it again, we may have to turn back."

"They already turned the lights out on the ground. Can you land in the dark?"

"I don't think I can even find the airstrip in the dark, much less land the plane."

He gripped the yoke more tightly. Muscles in his jaw bunched, as if he had gritted his teeth. We both knew we couldn't go back – there was no way to land without lights on the ground – so we had no choice but to press on and hope for sufficient clear space between the treetops of the Big Thicket and the cloud ceiling.

"So, anyway," Gabe said. He spoke with a nonchalant air, as if trying to calm me down, but I knew it was calculated to pacify both of us. He had his game face on but white knuckles betrayed his anxiety. "Why do good folks have to be hurt just so bad ones can be punished? And let's forget for a minute how often the bad go unpunished."

Return to the theological conversation drew my mind away from the potential danger we faced in the air and gave me something else to focus on. I trusted Gabe's piloting skills, so I left that in his hands.

"You ever play football?" I asked. I had, even earning an athletic scholarship to Southern Methodist University in Dallas after earning honorable mention all-district honors at Fort Worth's Polytechnic High School—"Poly" to those who went there, home of the Parrots. Unfortunately, my budding college football career at SMU was ended by a shattered ankle my freshman year. With football out of the picture and following a detour to Japan at the end of World War II, courtesy of the United States Army, I ultimately ended up at Baylor University where I studied to enter the ministry.

"Yeah," Gabe said, "I played in high school."

"You ever play in the rain?" Again, something I had experienced. In fact, I loved the rain because it turned our sparsely-vegetated high school fields to mud, which slowed the speed boys down to my level. I was a classic "mudder."

"Sure," Gabe said.

"Ever see it rain on the other side of the field, but not on your side?"

"Not once." He paused, then added, "I get your point."

I didn't even have to quote scripture to him. *Matthew 5:45: For he maketh His sun to rise on the evil and on the good, and sendeth the rain on the just and the unjust.*

"But we're not talking about rain on the gridiron," Gabe said after a moment of silence. "God ought to just put the ki-bosh on the ol' Devil and be done with it. If He's God, He can do that, right? If He couldn't, He wouldn't be God."

"In due time, Gabe. In due time."

Just then, we again disappeared into thick cloud cover. A sprinkling of rain pattered on the windshield.

"God's got impeccable timing, doesn't He?" Gabe said. "Or at least a sense of humor. Looks like it's raining on our side now."

He pushed the yoke forward; the nose of the plane dipped. After a few seconds, we broke free of the clouds again, but the sky around us had turned a gauzy whitish color. It was like flying through cotton candy.

Fog.

"That going to be a problem?" I asked. I knew he wasn't instrument-rated—he'd told me that before—and this seemed like the right time to follow up.

"As long as I can see, I can fly."

"Then I guess the question is, can you see?"

"Good enough." He paused, then added, "For now."

I leaned my head back against the headrest and closed my eyes. I hoped Gabe would think I was praying. That's what preachers do, don't they? Pray? Then again, I didn't want him to think I didn't trust his piloting skills. But my primary goal was simply to shut out the unpleasantness of flying blind. I'd rather not be able to see because my eyes were closed than not be able to see because of diminishing visibility. I felt like an ostrich and that if I stuck my head in the sand, I'd be safe. I figured what I couldn't see wouldn't hurt me, even if what I couldn't see was the fact that neither of us could see. At least not for much longer.

Exhaustion fused with tension and, before I knew it, I drifted off to sleep.

A sudden upthrust of the plane shook me awake. I opened my eyes but saw nothing through the windshield other than the thickness of fog, pressed around us in an embrace of wispy white. Visibility bad but at least not visibility zero.

The plane jumped upward again, accompanied by a loud

thumping sound beneath us. I heard the screech of something grating against metal, like giant fingernails on a blackboard. Then a series of ups and downs, as if something beneath was jabbing us in rhythm.

I looked at Gabe, whose hands squeezed the yoke, knuckles even whiter than before. Other than that, he looked perfectly composed. Just a pilot flying his aircraft. Or faking it for my benefit.

Another jolt.

"What is that?" I asked.

Gabe cut a quick glance my way, then eyes forward again. No answer.

"Gabe? What's going on?"

"Treetops."

"Treetops?"

"Treetops."

"Can't you go up?"

"I'm trying my best to stay level. Right now, I can't tell down from up. I couldn't even tell you if we're right-side up or upside down right now."

I had heard about that before, pilots becoming disoriented in fog and clouds. In fact, it was one of the reasons Gabe had wanted to avoid the low ceiling in the first place. It was the reason we were up there at that very moment, pitching around in the condition we tried to escape by leaving the night before we were scheduled.

"Treetops on the bottom of the plane mean we're upright, doesn't it?" I asked. "Otherwise, they'd be on the roof. So up is—" I jerked my thumb toward the ceiling. "—that way, isn't it?"

"You make a compelling argument," he said as he slowly eased back the yoke. The nose of the plane inched upward, but it seemed to me, as best I could see through the soup, that the right wing had dipped, rolling us toward the side.

"Your wing's down," I said.

He nodded again, adjusted the yoke again, and we seemed to level out. Or at least I thought we did. But then the wing seemed to dip once more. Suddenly we burst out of the fog into clear night air and both of us saw that the right wing was, indeed, dipping. Sharply. The plane banked in a circle, sometimes known as the "graveyard spiral." A continuous, descending circle pulling us into a funnel, like water down a drain. I didn't know how far above the treetops we were, but it couldn't have been far because, just moments earlier, they had been grabbing at our underside. Going down a drain seemed like an incredibly apt metaphor at that moment.

Gabe struggled with the yoke and, for a moment, I saw the right wing lift, if only slightly. And then we were right back in that thick soup.

That was the last clear memory I had of the flight.

CHAPTER TWO

"Preacher, get out. We've crashed."

Gabe's voice came from my left, sounding as if it came from a far distance.

I felt like I needed to shake my head, to clear out the cobwebs, but I knew it would rattle my brain around inside my skull like a BB in a box car. I lifted a hand to my forehead, gratified to find that my hand and arm responded to my instructions, further gratified that my head remained attached to my neck and shoulders. I felt no blood, another small blessing, I guess. Right then, I figured I'd take all the blessings I could get.

I slid my hand down and rubbed my eyes. I realized that my eyelids were closed, which explained the blackness. I tried to open them, but it seemed as if they were sealed shut. Using my fingers, I lifted the upper lids on both eyes and forced them open, one at a time. The blackness lifted. Through the cracked windshield in front of me, the moon's dim light in the depths of the forest revealed the trunk of a tree, at least two feet in diameter, scarcely five feet from the plane's nose. Five feet was all that separated us from a head-on collision that likely would have sealed our fate. Chalk up another one in the blessing category, though this one was a little bigger than a blood-free forehead.

I looked at Gabe, who struggled to extricate himself from the pilot's seat as the yoke pressed against him. His face appeared unmarked, matching mine, but I knew he was hurting just as I was.

"Where are we?" I asked.

"I don't know," he said. "Somewhere in the middle of the Thicket. We've got to get out."

"How? If we don't even know where we are."

"I'm talking about getting out of the plane. The fuel tanks are on the wings. Any kind of spark could set them off."

I looked out the window to my right, but I couldn't discern the outline of the wing. The shadows were too heavy. Still, getting out sounded like a good idea. I pushed the passenger door open and twisted my upper body to the side. But when I tried to step out, I couldn't move my legs. They obviously were pinned by the plane's nose having crumpled inward, much as Gabe was trapped by the yoke squeezing against him. He had, however, managed to throw his upper body out of the plane, with the door hanging open loosely from the impact. He slid out face first, then dragged his legs behind him.

"I'm trapped," I said.

"Wait a second and I'll come around to help."

He tried to stand, made it to his feet, then crumpled to the floor of the forest. "I think my legs are broken," he said.

"Hang on. Let me see if I can get out on my own."

I reached down to see what was pinning my legs, still unable to see clearly in the darkness. I felt something soft, which surprised me. I expected the cold metal of the dash, but this seemed more like the shape of a leg, specifically a thigh, then a knee. Though I could feel it with my hands, the object itself had no more sensation than a log.

I felt around in front of me with both hands. The dash, seemed intact, and the well of the passenger seat also seemed intact. That was when the truth dawned. There was no portion of the wreckage holding me inside; nothing pinning me to my seat. Nothing tangible to prevent me from getting out of the plane. I had simply lost the ability to move, or even to feel, my legs, though I could function with my arms and hands. I knew in that instant that I had broken my back. What I didn't know was whether I would ever walk again, though I figured that was a bridge I'd cross later. It remained to be seen whether I would cross it on foot or in a wheelchair. Or if I would ever cross any bridge at all.

"I can't move my legs," I said, but Gabe was already out of

my line of sight.

A rustling sound in leaves matting the forest floor pulled my attention away from myself for a minute. I looked out the open door, ready to grab the handle and pull it shut again should an animal materialize. After a few seconds, I saw Gabe's head appear as he crawled on his hands and knees around the open door and to my side.

"Did you say something?" he asked.

"I can't feel anything in my legs."

"Are you pinned in?"

"No. Just can't move my legs."

Rising on his knees, Gabe grabbed me around the waist with one arm, grabbed my inside shoulder with the other, and pulled my upper body out of the plane. It was just a short distance to the ground, and leaves padded my fall. He then tugged me until my legs fell lifelessly out of the doorway and onto the forest floor. It might have hurt under normal circumstances but I felt nothing below my waist.

I rolled onto my back and, using my elbows, inched my way up into a semi-sitting position, with my shoulders leaning against the fuselage of the wreckage. Gabe crawled next to me and sat, also leaning against the plane.

"At least we don't have to worry about fire," he said.

"Why's that?"

"Both wings are gone."

Which explained why I didn't see the one on my side when I looked earlier, though I had thought then I simply couldn't see it in the shadows.

"They must have been sheared off when we passed between a couple of trees," he said. "We got lucky. If they hadn't, we might have cartwheeled and, if we'd survived that, the fuel tanks might have exploded."

I notched another blessing in my mind. They seemed to be getting bigger and bigger. Add to that the fact that we were both still alive and it might even allow me to overlook that I was sitting on the floor of a forest, leaning against the wreckage of an airplane, without the use of my legs.

But no, it didn't quite do that. Yes, I was grateful to be alive, but I wasn't real sure that "it could have been worse" really counted as a blessing. If we ever made it out of there, that might make a good topic for a sermon someday. I had always thought that whether a glass was half-full or half-empty depended on whether you were filling or emptying it. But right then, I had no idea which I was doing. I also wondered if the glass had sprung a leak.

"Somebody'll come looking for us pretty soon, won't they?" I asked. But I already knew the answer before Gabe said it.

"They're not expecting us in Dallas until tomorrow. I didn't file a flight plan since we were leaving so late, so no one up there even knows we took off tonight."

And the only ones who did know, our friend from the church in Evadale who dropped us off at the airstrip, wouldn't have any reason to know we didn't make it home. If I'd been able to move my legs, I would have kicked myself for not calling Juanita to tell her we were leaving early. But it had been late by the time we finally decided to leave, and I hated to make a long distance collect call and wake the kids, who should have been in bed by 9:00.

It was starting to look like we were emptying a broken glass.

"Maybe someone heard us," I said. Even as I said it, I knew it sounded desperate.

"Maybe. We sure made enough noise, but I don't know how close we are to civilization. Woodville's probably the nearest town, but that could be five or ten miles from here. And even if someone did, no one's going to head off into the Thicket at night just because they think they heard a noise."

"How about the radio?"

"I tried before I got out. It's dead."

"Not much of an optimist, are you?"

Gabe smiled. A sad smile. "I'm more of a realist. And I'd say it's still raining cats and dogs on our side of the field right now."

We sat silently for a few moments, leaning against the wreckage of the plane. The metal chilled my back. I wore a suit coat and Gabe had a leather flight jacket, but that wasn't much protection for a January night in the deep heart of a forest. Temperatures weren't typically frigid in that part of the state this time of year, although it had been close to 50 degrees when we took off and the weather forecast called for overnight lows in the mid-to-lower-40s. But that was for the towns and cities. Out here, I figured upper 30s wasn't out of the question. What was certain was that it would be a cold night and we were ill-equipped to deal with it.

As time passed, I saw that Gabe was growing weaker, floating in and out of consciousness. I had confirmed that both his legs were broken below the knees, something that was evident even to a layman by touch. There were no other outward signs of trauma, but he complained of pain throughout his torso, suggesting significant internal injuries. He slid to a prone position, rather than continuing to lean against the fuselage, to take off some of the pressure. I feared that he wouldn't survive the night. All I could do was try to keep him comfortable and awake as he lay there. I was afraid that if he fell asleep, he might never wake up.

When the cold set in, a somewhat dramatic drop in temperature over the course of less than an hour, I crawled to the door of the plane. "Crawl" was not exactly accurate, because getting up on my hands and knees for the traditional version of crawling was out of the question. Instead, I used my elbows to pull my upper body forward and drag my lower body, inching along until I reached the door. I raised up as far as I could and fumbled around behind the passenger seat for our luggage.

In Gabe's backpack, I found a change of clothes, a smashed thermos, a pack of cigarettes, and a cigarette lighter. I slipped the backpack over one shoulder then grabbed my briefcase from behind the passenger seat and worked my way back to his side.

It was just a matter of a few feet, but I when I reached him, I felt as if I had just run a marathon. Gabe was unconscious, so I draped a flannel shirt I found in his bag across his chest and tucked it in around his sides. He never moved.

I leaned close to ensure his other side was covered and that was when I noticed that he didn't appear to be breathing.

"Gabe," I said. I grabbed him by the chin and gently shook. "Gabe."

No response. I touched the side of his neck for a pulse but felt nothing. I checked again, this time on his wrist. Still nothing. I leaned down and turned my head, placing my ear next to his nose and listened for sounds of breathing. Once more, nothing. I was no doctor but the conclusion was inescapable.

While it might have been too early to fully panic just a couple of hours ago, even though panic had gained a toehold, it now seemed ripe for a full-blown panic attack. I lay on the floor of the Big Thicket, at night, in the dead of winter, next to a wrecked airplane with a dead radio, a dead pilot, and a broken back, unable to walk and barely able to crawl. There was no one even aware that we had left Evadale, much less that we had crashed, and no one to miss us for probably another eighteen hours. Yeah, if that wasn't the perfect time to panic, I didn't know when was.

I rolled onto my back and lay next to Gabe. Tried to think. To come up with some kind of a plan. I closed my eyes, a little unsure if I should, for fear I'd never be able to open them again.

And I prayed. Prayed like I'd never prayed before.

Prayed as if my life depended on it. And it probably did. But what to ask for? Heal my back so I could get on my feet and walk out of there? Raise Gabe from the dead, like Lazarus, and put the wings back on the plane so he could fly us out of there? Come to someone in a dream and tell them there's a wrecked plane in the middle of the Big Thicket and to send help?

None of those sounded realistic, although I knew that wasn't the criteria. I had always believed that God was the God of miracles. Hadn't He, through His son, made the blind to see, the deaf to hear, and the dumb to speak? Hadn't He made the lame to walk—and boy, didn't that sound good right now? To get up and walk? And hadn't He raised the dead, turned water into wine, fed five thousand with a few measly fish and loaves of bread? Hadn't He walked on water?

Still, asking for a miracle for myself somehow seemed selfish, though who could blame me? I figured God probably wouldn't begrudge me that, given my circumstance. After all, I had a wife and three young kids back at home who needed me, so it wouldn't really be selfish, would it?

Then a prayer came to me that offered comfort in my personal storm. A prayer as simple as, "I trust my situation to you. Thy will be done."

As I spoke those words aloud, I heard a faint noise in the distance.

I squeezed my already closed eyes tighter and strained to listen. It was the first sound I had heard since the crash, but this was also the first time I forced myself to shut out the roar in my head and to listen. The sound was unmistakable.

Traffic on a road. A truck, maybe. Something big. Somewhere close, although the way sound traveled at night made it difficult to tell. Besides, given my inability to walk, it might as well have been a thousand miles away. And then it was gone, as the vehicle drove past and presumably disappeared down a highway somewhere in the dark.

For the first time in what seemed like a long while, or at least since we had crashed, I felt a sense of hope. I would have to depend on my sense of hearing, but I figured if there was one vehicle on that road, surely others would come along. There might not be many until morning, but if I could make it through the night, and if I could pinpoint the direction from which the traffic sounds came, then I at least had a goal. A plan. Having a plan was half the battle. Call it crawling, or simply dragging my body, or wriggling, call it what you will, but I would make my way to that road. I *would* get to that road.

That is, if I actually survived the night. That was the first big *if*, and it was no "gimme." For starters, to do that, I had to keep from freezing to death. I knew of course, that the temperatures weren't actually freezing, though it felt like it. And who knew what the darkest hours of the night would hold? I had to find some way to stay warm.

I looked at my companion's body lying prone on the forest floor. He still wore his leather flight jacket, while all I had was a thin suit coat. That jacket sure looked warm. And Gabe sure didn't need it anymore.

As soon as it popped into my head, I shook the thought away. That was Gabe's jacket. It would be too much like cannibalism, stripping the dead of his belongings. I couldn't do that.

I wouldn't do that. I would find another way to stay warm. I had an idea.

I rose on one elbow and swept out a clearing in the leaves, right down to the dirt. About a yard in diameter. Next, I created a small pile of leaves in the middle of the clearing. I opened my briefcase and emptied it. From a notebook of sermon notes, I extracted several pages and crumpled them into paper balls, then dropped them back into the now empty briefcase. I scraped up a few handfuls of leaves and placed them on top of the paper. I hoped the briefcase would provide a second buffer, along with the clearing I had created, from other dried leaves.

I grasped the cigarette lighter I found in Gabe's backpack and clicked it a few times, but with no success. I figured I could be forgiven for my clumsiness with the lighter. After all, I didn't smoke—that would be frowned on in a Baptist preacher—so why would I be expected to be an expert with a lighter?

After a few more tries, though, I managed to create a small flicker of a flame. Holding it to the crumpled notes, I started a small fire. Small enough to keep it under control—after all, I didn't want to start a forest fire that I couldn't run away from; wouldn't that be ironic?—but just big enough to throw off a tiny bit of heat. I couldn't keep it going long, but maybe just long enough to warm my hands and face and allow me to sleep once it went out.

"I'll bet that's the hottest your sermons have ever been."

The voice startled me. It sounded like Gabe, but he still lay, unmoving, beside me on the ground.

I looked around, searching for the source of the voice.

"That fire's not gonna do it," the voice said. Boy, it sure did sound like Gabe. "You better take my jacket."

I peered into the darkness and barely made out the shape of a man, leaning against the nose of the plane. He walked closer, then squatted next to Gabe's body.

I couldn't believe my eyes. Surely, I was hallucinating.

It was Gabe. Next to Gabe. Two Gabes. One dead; one alive. Or one a ghost. Crazy!

"What was it James Dean said?" ghost Gabe asked. "Live fast, die young, and leave a good-looking corpse?"

He felt for a pulse on dead Gabe and shook his head. "Already cold."

He stood and took off his jacket, then offered it to me. "I don't need it anymore," he said.

Now I knew I was hallucinating. Ghosts didn't wear jackets, did they?

"Come on, take it," Ghost Gabe said.

I reached out and accepted it from him. It felt soft and pliable, the leather conditioned by years of wear. Tangible. It was as real as any jacket I ever felt.

I struggled to get up on my elbows, then scooted back further against the plane. It took considerable effort to balance myself but I managed to lean forward and put the jacket on over my suit coat. I zipped it to the top. It fit a little snugly, but at least it fit.

"Thank—"

I couldn't even get the "you" out when I looked up and saw that Ghost Gabe who had offered me the jacket was gone. But the dead Gabe, lying on the ground, was still there. Only now he wasn't wearing his jacket.

Had I taken it off his body? I didn't remember doing so but, cannibalism or not, obviously I had. First hallucinating, and now memory loss. More memory loss, I should say. I still couldn't find those missing few minutes just before the crash. I added reasons for full panic to my lengthening list.

I shifted farther back toward the plane until my back rested fully against it, my dead legs stretched in front of me. I took the broken thermos from Gabe's backpack, tilted my head back, and held it over my mouth. A few drops of cold coffee trickled out.

I unzipped the flight jacket and took my handkerchief from the inner breast pocket of my suit coat. I balled the end of it and swabbed the interior of the thermos for any remnants of liquid. I put the balled end of the handkerchief in my mouth and sucked on it, extracting a last bit of coffee.

"Don't you know coffee'll kill you?"

Again, Gabe's voice startled me. I checked, and he still lay dead on the forest floor.

I heard rustling of leaves, like footsteps, then Ghost Gabe appeared at the nose of the plane, walking around and examining the wreckage. Jacketless, he stopped and looked down at me.

"Jacket fits you pretty good," he said. "You almost look like a pilot instead of a preacher."

He gestured with his thumb at dead Gabe. "You sure look better than him." He laughed and added, "Or me, I guess I should say."

He laughed again, and I joined in. It seemed ridiculous but I couldn't help myself. He was a funny ghost. Or so I thought in my pain-addled head.

Gabe winced and folded his arms across his ribs. "Too soon to laugh, I guess. Hurts."

"Do ghosts feel pain?" I asked.

"Who says I'm a ghost? Maybe I'm just a hallucination."

"Or maybe you're an angel."

"Whatever floats your boat, preacher."

"Bad metaphor. Wouldn't the wind beneath my wings be better?"

He laughed, then squeezed his ribs again. "You're killing me."

He gestured towards the body lying next to me. "Too late. Looks like I'm already gone."

He turned and pointed at me. "You're going to be, too, if you don't get out of here."

"That's the plan." I said. "At first light. I'm going to head in the direction of that traffic I've been hearing."

"Think you'll last 'til morning?"

"What choice do I have? It's too dark. Besides—"

"Besides, what?"

"Now that I think about it, maybe I shouldn't venture off too far. I've always heard it's better to stay with the plane."

"And this is based on your years of experience with plane crashes? How many you been in before this?"

"None. Then again, I never flew with you before."

"Oh, that hurts." He winced. "Literally."

"I read books," I said. "I watch television. It just makes sense. Won't it be easier for a search party to spot a plane than to spot a man on the ground in this thicket?"

Gabe considered that, then said, "It might be. If there was anyone looking. By the time anyone misses us, you'll be laid out like me, there."

"Maybe I'll just have to get someone's attention."

I grabbed a broken branch lying next to my legs. Holding it in my right hand, I swung it around my body and banged it into the side of the fuselage. The hollow metallic sound seemed deafening in my ears. If there was a road nearby, I thought, maybe there were homes nearby, too. With people inside. People with ears.

I banged it again. And again. The sound reverberated and echoed in the stillness of the night.

"Do you really think anyone can hear that?" Gabe asked.

"Who knows?" I swung the branch again.

"We're all alone out here, preacher. The only ones who'll hear that—"

I swung again.

"—are the animals."

I stopped my arm in mid-air, like a one-armed baseball slugger checking his swing.

"Wild hogs, coyotes, bobcats," Gabe said. "I've heard tell there used to be black bears and wolves around here. Not anymore, I don't think, but there might still be a panther or two."

"Panthers?"

"That's what I've heard. They scream, high-pitched, just like a woman. It'll make your blood run cold. If I were you, I wouldn't want to be lying there if one should come along. I'd want to be moving."

"What difference would it make if I'm lying here or lying out there, somewhere? You overestimate my ability to move quickly."

Gabe threw up his hands and shook his head. "No, you're right. You're right. Forget I said anything. You're fine here. This is as good a place to die as any."

He turned away and walked toward the trees. I watched until he had faded into the shadows. Some angel, I thought. Thanks for the support.

As he faded, I heard a strange exchange of voices in my head, ones I had never heard before, but I knew the context. Scripture I had read dozens of times over the years. About a heavenly meeting, one where God challenged Satan with the faith of his servant Job.

"Hast thou considered my servant Job, that there is none like him in the earth, a perfect and upright man, one that feareth God and escheweth evil?"

And Satan responded, *"Doth Job fear God for naught? Take away your blessing, and he will curse thee to thy face."*

Lying there on the floor of the Big Thicket, cold and scared, I still had my list of small blessings, but I wondered if God was withdrawing His big blessing. If so, would I curse God to His face? The truth was, I didn't know.

Asashio Taro III reigned as a sumo champion in Japan in a career that started in the late 1940s and ended in the early 1960s, attaining the ultimate rank of Yokozuna in March of 1959, the 46th Yokozuna in sumo history. During the five years the Farris family spent in Japan as missionaries, from 1958 to 1963, Asashio dominated the sport and piqued my interest. I was never able to see him wrestle in person, but watched him on occasion on Japanese television, usually with Mike, my elder son, beside me.

Born Michael David Farris in 1955, he was just shy of three years old when the Farris family sailed to Japan to begin our adventure as missionaries. We called him Corky Bo, which started off as Corky Boy, so dubbed by friends and family of Juanita's and mine who made a play on my name. But he had trouble pronouncing it when he was learning to talk and it came out Corky Bo. The nickname stuck.

Besides Asashio's skill in the sumo ring and his massive size, particularly for a Japanese—records show that he stood six feet

*two inches and weighed, in his prime, just shy of 300 pounds—
he was most noted for incredibly thick black eyebrows, which
gave him a particularly fierce appearance. And Corky Bo was
as captivated by Asashio's appearance as I was by his athletic
skill.*

*One early evening, after we had moved to the northern
Japan island of Hokkaido, I needed to leave the house for a
meeting at the local Baptist church in Sapporo. In the winter,
days were short on Hokkaido, with the sun setting as early as
4:00 in the afternoon, so it was dark outside that evening as I
prepared to leave. Thick clouds promised yet more snow in a
city that could easily see upwards of 100 inches of snowfall
annually.*

Corky Bo, now about five years old, was worried about me.

*"Daddy, don't go," he said, with as much earnestness as a
five-year-old was capable of mustering. "It's dark outside."*

"I know son, but it'll be all right."

"But it's really dark."

"I know, but you don't need to worry about me."

*"But Daddy," he said, exasperation now mixed with fear in
his voice. "It's darker than Asashio's eyebrows."*

There had been a bit of moon visible when Gabe and I had
taken off earlier from Evadale but lying there next to my dead
friend on the floor of the Big Thicket, fog and treetops
obliterated the moon and blackened the sky. I knew that
darkness was a metaphor in the Bible for Satan and his evil
forces, and there I was, lying in darkness.

Darker than Asashio's eyebrows.

CHAPTER THREE

January 13, 1965

I didn't know how I managed to sleep—hurt, cold, scared, and on hard ground—but somehow, I did. Nor did I know when my tiny fire died out, but fortunately I had contained it to the small clearing so that it didn't spread and engulf me in a forest fire overnight. Small blessings, again.

When I awoke the next morning, the sun's rays had not fully found their way to the forest floor, but at least they had chased away some of the gloom of night. Not the cold, though. I felt a chill from head to . . . well, not to toe. In fact, from the waist down, I didn't feel anything. I would have welcomed that chill in my legs, but it was not to be. My upper body sure felt the temperature, though.

I looked over at Gabe, who still lay motionless on the ground beside me. Still unjacketed. I checked my watch: 7:20 in the morning. Remarkably, the watch hadn't broken in the crash; not even the face of it was cracked, and it still kept perfect time. If I ever got out of there alive, I would contact the Timex company and offer it up for another television commercial narrated by John Cameron Swayze. I could almost hear his voice in my head: "The plane went down in the Big Thicket of Texas, crushing its owner's back. But incredibly, his watch is still working after taking that punishment. Timex takes a licking and keeps on ticking."

Of course, that all depended on whether or not I kept on ticking. I thought the watch faced better odds than I did. Mine were decreasing by the hour.

As I regained my senses, I took note of other aspects of my condition besides being cold. My stomach growled, but there was nothing to eat. My throat was dry, but there was nothing to drink, either. I knew I could live without food for a while, maybe even weeks, but conventional wisdom I had heard my whole life said that a person could survive only about three days without water. I didn't know whether that was true or not since conventional wisdom was notoriously unreliable. All I really knew was that I was incredibly thirsty. The last moisture I had taken in was the remnants of cold coffee from Gabe's thermos. It would still be hours before we were reported missing, and I decided that I needed to start moving, if for no other reason than to locate a water source.

I dragged myself back to the passenger door of the wreckage again, looking for supplies. I took a white button-down dress shirt from my small suitcase I had stashed behind the passenger seat, and a flashlight and a Texas map from the floor of the cabin. If I was able to get my bearings from the sun, I might be able to locate the highway I heard traffic on last night and be able to pinpoint, generally, where I was. At a minimum, I could then figure out in which direction to go.

I leaned my back against the nose of the plane, my useless legs splayed in front of me, and opened the map on my lap. Shadows made it difficult to see so I held it close to my face and squinted.

"Maps are good."

It was Gabe. I didn't know where he came from but he was suddenly right there. Hallucination, ghost, or angel—and I was pretty well ready to write off the last one, given his obnoxious attitude—he seemed to come and go as he pleased. Must be nice.

He squatted next to me and took the map. Actually held it in his hands. Giving away jackets and touching paper maps, he was challenging all my preconceived notions about ghosts.

"I wondered when you'd be back to pronounce me dead," I said. "Sorry to disappoint you, but I'm still alive and kicking." I paused and looked at my legs. "Maybe not kicking."

"At least you haven't lost your sense of humor."

"It may be all I've got left."

"Jacket keep you warm?"

"Good enough," I said. "Thanks."

"Don't mention it. What's with the map?"

"I've been thinking about what you said last night, and I'm back to my original plan. I've got to get out of here. I can't wait any longer."

"That's good," he said. He handed the map back to me. "Shows initiative. There's just one problem with the map, though."

"What's that?"

"There's no 'you are here' arrow on it. Map's useless without that. You can't figure out where to go unless you know where you're starting from."

"You're the guy who was driving the airplane last night. You tell me where we are."

"Kinda dark last night."

"So how do I figure it out?"

"You need to start with a landmark," he said.

"There's a road or highway out there somewhere. I can hear it."

We both went silent and listened. Gabe cocked his head like a dog, then shook it.

"I don't hear anything. You're hallucinating."

"I figure that's why I can see you. And I didn't say it was a well-traveled road. But I'm sure I heard traffic last night."

"As sure as you can see me?"

"If you can believe in yourself, why can't you believe in my road?"

"Point taken." He held out his hand. "Give me the map again."

I handed it to him, and he spread it on the ground. He moved his finger over a dark green area of southeast Texas.

"That's the Big Thicket," he said. "Over there is Woodville.

Down here is Evadale, where we took off. On the north end up there is State Highway 190, that runs between Woodville and Livingston. Highway 69 runs north from Beaumont to Woodville and splits the Thicket. You've also got a farm-to-market road that runs southeast to northwest and hooks into 190. Those are the three most likely choices."

"Okay."

"What kind of traffic did you hear?"

"What do you mean?"

"Trucks or cars?"

"I only heard one. It sounded like a truck, but I can't be sure. Kinda loud. And I think it was going pretty fast, whatever it was."

"Those farm-to-market roads get plenty dark at night, and that tends to slow drivers down. I'm guessing that means it was probably a highway. And based on the direction we were headed when we went down, we should be at the north end of Thicket. That puts us near 190. I'd say you want to keep going north."

"Then that's the direction I'll go."

"You sure you're up to it?"

"What do you mean?"

"I've been watching you crawl around here since last night, and you don't exactly inspire confidence."

I shook my head, trying to chase away this version of Gabe Rogers. The one last night seemed gung ho for me to get started and now, all of a sudden, he had turned into Timmy Timid.

"What's gotten into you, anyway?" I asked. "Now you want me to quit? Well, I don't quit."

"Maybe I'm just coming to my senses. Or maybe you sold me last night. You can be pretty persuasive. What if they come looking and find the plane, but can't find you? What'll you do then?"

"Aren't you the one who said they wouldn't even start looking until the middle of the day? Maybe even later? You're confusing me."

"I just want to be sure you know what you're doing. I've seen this before. Someone gets a sudden burst of courage and ends up making things worse for themselves. That's all."

I could feel my temper rising. Who was this guy—this dead guy—trying to tell me what to do? This didn't sound at all like the Gabe I talked to last night.

Or did I really talk to anybody last night? I had already written off the theory that he was an angel, and a ghost was also seeming unlikely. Maybe he really was just a hallucination, after all. So, was I simply talking to myself, arguing with myself? My rational self versus my idealistic, rose-colored-glasses self? I liked my optimistic self, and I even liked my rational self. But this version left something to be desired. If this was me, dressed up as Gabe, I was giving myself no quarter. Seems I could be kind of a jerk.

"Believe me, preacher," he said, "it's one thing to be brave when you're nice and safe, but it's different when you're going through the valley of the shadow of death. And if you don't think this is that valley, just take a look at ol' Gabe over there, lying next to you."

"I know a little something about the Twenty-third Psalms," I said. "You don't think I can practice what I preach?"

"I don't think you've seen the ball since kick-off. Nothing personal, preacher, but you showed your true colors when you were whining about not being found if you left the plane. If God unleashes a rainstorm on your side of the field, I'll give you until the end of the first quarter to call it quits."

If this was one of my alter egos, I couldn't believe how hard I was being on myself. I knew now, for sure, that this wasn't Gabe speaking. Gabe was kind and supportive, not anything like this jerk in the woods. Was that really me?

"Do me a favor," I said. "Just go be dead. I'll take care of this on my own. Like I said, I don't quit. I never quit."

"Fine by me."

"I'm not the one who got us into this. I wasn't driving the airplane."

"Fine. You're on your own."

He started off toward the trees. I looked at the map, then up in search of the sun, but I couldn't see it through the treetops.

I tossed the map aside and called after Gabe, who had already faded from view.

"Wait! Which way is north?"

Didn't Boy Scouts learn something about how to find north? Too bad I was never a Boy Scout.

"Gabe!" I called. "Which way is north?"

All I got was silence.

CHAPTER FOUR

With my mind made up, and warmed by Gabe's leather jacket, I readied myself to leave the relative security of the plane wreckage. It was funny to think of it as security, but it had at least offered some measure of protection when we dove nose first onto the floor of the Thicket. It contained what might well be the last of my worldly goods should the worst happen, and it even might offer shelter should the weather turn sour. More sour, that is, than had already forced us down.

It was also the place where my companion lay, his body damaged and unmoving. Still, it was what my world had narrowed to, and to leave it and set off into the midst of the Big Thicket, not knowing what I might face or where I might end up—well, I don't mind telling you, that was a very unsettling thought. My nightmare scenario was that our wreckage was spotted by rescuers in the air, who then sent a ground crew to the battered fuselage, only to find a dead pilot and a missing preacher. What if I got so far away that I couldn't see them? Or they couldn't see me, not even a white shirt being waved in the air? Or couldn't hear me?

What if I encountered a wild hog or a bobcat? Worse yet, a panther? An unarmed two-legged man stood little chance against a wild animal, and an unarmed paralyzed man stood none. Not while lying prone on the forest floor, unable to move or defend himself from attack.

Those possible outcomes if I left the wreckage seemed dire, but the alternative seemed worse. Rescuers would have to start with an aerial search, which itself might be a nearly impossible task. What if I waited by the plane for rescue, and it never came, while there was a reachable highway with traffic nearby? Could the wreckage be seen from the air, lying crumpled at the feet of trees that towered as high as 100 or 150 feet?

Could a land search be any more successful, assuming a

targeted area could be narrowed down? I knew that there were tens of thousands of acres of forested land in the Big Thicket, maybe even as much as eighty or one hundred thousand acres. That was somewhere in the range of 125 to 160 square miles of heavily forested land, with tangles of underbrush and fallen trees that would make a coordinated grid search a nearly impossible task with anything less than a platoon of searchers.

That was assuming that a search started with the Big Thicket, which was no guarantee. Because we hadn't filed a flight plan, no one knew for sure the route we had taken last night. Logic might dictate that we went down in the Big Thicket, since it was closest to Evadale, but no one would know how soon after take-off we went down. North of the Thicket lay Angelina National Forest, another 150,000 acres of pine forest, an additional 230 square miles. If searchers thought we had ventured a little more to the west as we headed north, to take a more direct route toward Dallas, we would have passed over Davy Crockett National Forest, 160,000 additional acres, or 250 square miles.

Someone might even consider that, given the low fog ceiling last night, we might have started out west toward Interstate 45, which connected Houston with Dallas, so we could follow the lights of the freeway north. Had we done that, we would have passed over Sam Houston National Forest, yet another 160,000 acres.

And none of those possibilities took into account the fact that no one would think to start looking, in the first place, until probably mid-afternoon, which offered limited hours of daylight to search, since sunset occurred close to 5:00 p.m. The bottom line was that even if an air search began as early as noon—and that was a stretch—the odds of our being discovered by sunset were virtually nil. I had Gabe's cigarette lighter tucked into his jacket pocket but spending another cold night and trying to start a small fire on the forest floor did not appeal. If I wanted to be found, I had to get out of there. I had to get to a road or a house.

I had to move.

As the sun got higher in the sky, creating a few breaks in the shadows, the highway I detected last night began to take on sounds of life. I heard the occasional car passing, even a truck or two. I had no idea how far off, but if I could just make it out of the trees and onto a roadside, if I could just reach that highway, I stood a chance. A small chance but still a chance. It was time to go.

CHAPTER FIVE

I tucked the white button-down dress shirt, along with the flashlight and map, into Gabe's backpack. I hoped I wouldn't need the flashlight, because that would mean the passage of another day without rescue. The shirt would serve a dual purpose. Extra warmth, if need be, but also something to catch the eye of rescuers. My hope was to be discovered before the sun set again, and the white shirt would be visible if I waved it. But that thought begged the question: Visible to whom? Or to what? I preferred to think about the whom and not the what.

Just as I slung the backpack over my shoulder, no easy task while essentially lying prone on the ground, I heard the sound of an engine. A big engine. A plane of some sort, most likely military, shuttling between any of the number of military bases in this part of the state. It was way too loud to be another small plane like ours, and too low to be a large passenger jetliner. Not this far away from any major airport that served aircraft of that type, the closest being Houston, over 100 miles away. The only thing closer was probably the municipal airport in Beaumont, which serviced smaller aircraft. If what I was hearing was, in fact, a passenger carrier flying that low, I worried that it might reach the same fate as befell our small Mooney, ripping off tree-tops before plunging to the floor of the forest.

But at least that might send rescuers my way.

As soon as it crossed my mind, I banished the thought. I wouldn't wish my fate on anyone else.

A staticky voice chirped from the cabin of the plane. Looking around, I couldn't see anything that might be the source. Not even Gabe. Then it hit me. The radio may have seemed dead the night before, but it obviously still worked, at least well enough to receive, though maybe not able to send.

I rolled over onto my stomach. The wreckage of the fuselage was close, maybe no more than ten feet or so. If I could just get there in time. And if the radio would send.

If, if, if.

I reached forward with one elbow and dug my fingers into the dirt. I tried to get on my knees, to attain a traditional crawling posture, like a baby, but my lower body refused to obey the commands from my brain. I had no ability to raise my pelvic region or to draw my legs up beneath me. I couldn't even bend them, to create a ninety-degree angle at my knees. They were useless. Totally useless. Nothing but dead weight trailing in my wake.

I reached my other elbow forward and dug into the dirt again, then lowered both forearms and grabbed dirt with both hands. With my arms fully extended, my face pressed against the ground and fingertips dug in, I pulled, as if doing a horizontal pull-up. I tried to raise my head, to keep from burrowing my nose in dirt as I felt my body inch forward, toward the radio. The voice was still there, growing louder.

Then a shadow loomed overhead. I rolled to my side and looked up at the belly of a large, gray-bodied C-130 Hercules, a four-engine turboprop military transport aircraft, as it passed overhead. Its engines drowned out any sound from the radio; its draft stirred tree branches and raised dust devils out of leaves. I raised my white shirt over my head and waved it, but I was too hidden by trees, the plane was too high, and then it was too late.

Then it was gone, out of sight, even out of sound. And with it, the last vestiges of the voice on the radio. As the voice faded out, my own last vestige—that of hope—disappeared.

"Think he saw you?"

Gabe, back to taunt, I was sure. He appeared at the nose of the plane. He leaned against it and studied me.

"Maybe," I said, though I didn't believe it. "He was flying pretty low."

"Not that low. He had to stay way above those treetops."

"That might have been good advice to follow last night."

"Ouch," Gabe said. "I thought preachers were supposed to turn the other cheek."

"Just pointing out the obvious. Besides, turning the other cheek is one thing. Being a punching bag is something entirely different."

"Point taken. But while we're pointing out the obvious, it didn't look like you were having that much luck getting to the radio."

"The radio that's not dead."

"Missed the point again. My question is this: Just how far do you think you'll get pulling yourself along like that? Man, it was painful to watch."

I had been on my side as we talked, but now I rolled over onto my back. Easier to make eye contact with him.

"Farther than if I don't try at all," I said. "But now, I've got a question for you."

"Fire away."

"You seem to be able to come and go as you please. You keep disappearing and then showing up again. Where do you go?"

"Maybe I don't go anywhere. Maybe I'm still here, tethered to my body, and you just can't see me. You know, if I'm a ghost and all. Or maybe I'm tethered to my plane. Wouldn't that be something? Either way, it doesn't really make much difference, does it?"

I hadn't thought about that. I didn't know enough about ghosts to know what the rules were. I wasn't even sure I believed in them, at all. But I'd seen enough movies to know that, if they existed, they haunted places that meant something to them, even if their bodies were buried in a cemetery far away. So, it made sense that maybe he was haunting his plane.

And if he was simply a hallucination, and not a ghost, then he was likely tethered to my imagination and not free to wander around outside of my imaginatory jurisdiction. That meant he would go with me as far as I could go. Part of me thought I might enjoy the company, but he still needed an attitude adjustment.

Then again, what if he was an angel? At first thought, that seemed unlikely. If he was, he was sure a sarcastic, somewhat hateful angel, which seemed out of character for angels. I was still in the early stages of my ministry—hadn't even been out of the seminary seven years—and not altogether up on angels just yet. I knew, though, that while the Bible was a bit light on specifics about angels, they seemed to be jacks-of-all-trades. They could be guardians, messengers, even avengers.

I didn't know if Gabe's attitude disqualified him as one or not. But if he were an angel, could he find help for me? Or was his role simply limited to comforting me in my final hours? If it was the latter, giving comfort, he didn't seem to be very good at it.

He also didn't seem to be a very good guardian. If he had been, I wouldn't be crawling around on my belly in the woods. But what if he was an avenging angel, sent to punish me for disobeying God? I'd have to think about that one. It might explain his caustic attitude. The problem with his being an avenger, though, was that as far as I knew, I was in God's will.

Or was I?

I decided there was one way to start eliminating options for what Gabe was or wasn't. I would head out, away from the plane, and see if he followed me. If he didn't, or couldn't, that might suggest he was a ghost, shackled to the wreckage of his plane. If he did, or could, then I had at least narrowed it down to hallucination or angel. I'd figure out something later to help me decide between those two. Maybe a coin toss.

I rolled over onto my stomach and made sure the backpack was secure on my shoulder. Then I reached forward again, but this time I bent my forearm back toward my head so that I dug in solely with my elbow. As I pulled forward with my elbow, my upper body raised a bit, bending backward at my waist. I reached with my other elbow and pulled again. I found that I got a better grip this way than with my fingers and that each pull gained me anywhere from eight to ten inches. Progress.

But not much.

I still wasn't sure how far away the highway sounds were, but I did a rough calculation in my head. If the highway was a mile away, that was a little over 63,000 inches. If each elbow pull averaged nine inches, that was about 7,000 pulls. If I averaged five elbow pulls per minute, that was 1,400 minutes, which was nearly 24 hours.

So, back to the if, if, if. If I could keep up that pace, and if the highway was truly just a mile away, it would take me a full day to reach it. If I didn't die first. Another if.

But what if it turned out that the highway was more than a mile away? Worse yet, what if my hallucinations included hearing traffic sounds that really didn't exist, and there was no highway at all? Then what?

I decided that it was better to just throw in the towel, stay here, and wait it out.

I heard that voice again. *"Does Job serve God for naught?"* Then it repeated, but this time it said, *"Does Corky Farris serve God for naught?"*

That brought back the nagging question that had plagued me earlier: Was I really in God's will?

Then a scripture popped into my head, one I had preached before. *Jeremiah 12:5: If thou hast run with the footmen, and they have wearied thee, then how canst thou contend with horses? And if in the land of peace, wherein thou trustedst, they wearied thee, then how wilt thou do in the swelling of Jordan?*

Up until now, I'd had my share of difficulties and tragedies. I had lost loved ones, had suffered financial setbacks, had undergone illnesses, and had seen family members suffer from illnesses. I felt like I had weathered all those things just fine. But maybe I had just been running with the footmen then, and now I had to contend with horses. Maybe this was my swelling of Jordan.

But what if this was still just running with footmen? What if God was merely preparing me to contend with the horses? What if the real swelling of Jordan was yet to come? Either way, I decided that I wasn't ready to give up. Not just yet.

I ran a new calculation in my head. If I reached a little farther with my elbows, I could pull twelve inches each time. And if I worked a little harder, I could do eight per minute. Run the numbers and now you were looking at eleven hours. Remarkable! I had cut the time more than in half and I hadn't even started. I was burning daylight.

CHAPTER SIX

I didn't know how long I'd been crawling, if you could call it that, but it seemed like it had been for hours. Every time I dug an elbow into the ground and pulled, it felt as if I were doing pull-ups while bearing a 100 pound backpack. My arm and upper back muscles screamed in agony but, frankly, I preferred that to the nothingness I felt in my legs dragging uselessly behind me.

When I felt as if I could go no farther, I rolled onto my back for a brief respite. I was exhausted, more tired than any football practice or even the United States Army's torture at Camp Hood called "basic training." "Basic" apparently meant "how far can a human being be pushed." But I would have traded what I was experiencing on the floor of the woods in January for the worst of those training days, or two-a-day football practices, in the Texas summer heat.

I couldn't remember the last time I looked at my watch, nor what time I had actually gotten started, but I remembered the position of the sun when I left, so I looked skyward. Judging from what little sun I could make out overhead through the trees, and how far it had – or hadn't – moved since I started, it hadn't been nearly as long as it felt like. Certainly not hours; maybe more like thirty minutes. But each of those minutes were starting to feel sorta like dog years. Like thirty minutes of real time equals two-and-a-half hours of paralyzed crawling time.

I rolled onto my side and folded my hands under the side of my head as I lay in a thick carpet of leaves. My shoulders ached and my neck hurt from holding up my head as I crawled. I felt a doozy of a headache coming on and longed for a glass of water and an aspirin.

I shifted my body around and looked back at the crooked path I had traversed. By bending my trail around tree trunks, not to mention that even my straight lines were more zig-zag than straight, I had probably covered at least three or four times more distance than a true straight line would have taken me. Looking back and sighting along that line, I could see the wreckage of the fuselage no more than maybe twenty yards or so away. I could still see Gabe's body laid out beside his plane, still not moving. I could see I was going to have to run a whole new set of distance/time calculations in my head. Either that or search-and-rescue teams were going to need to double-time it. Or triple-time it.

"I've seen little old ladies make better time."

Gabe's voice came from overhead. I rolled onto my back, the backpack forcing my shoulders upward, and looked at him. He sat on a tree branch about ten feet off the ground, directly above my head, his legs and boots dangling below him. He wore the same cocky grin he had the last time I had seen him – thirty minutes or so before.

"And I've seen those same little old ladies fly better," I said.

"Glad to see you haven't lost your sense of humor."

"So happy I can please you."

He grabbed the limb on both sides of his body, swung his legs out, and dropped to the ground, landing noisily in the dry leaves. Did ghosts or hallucinations make noise?

He kicked around at the debris surrounding him, clearing a small area.

"You looking for something?" I asked.

"Snakes."

And now, so was I. I didn't figure I'd be able to scamper up that tree if one appeared.

"Don't snakes hibernate in cold weather?" I asked.

"Not really. They sleep, and get kinda sluggish, but it's not a true hibernation. They do look for warm places to sleep, though, and a pile of leaves would fit the bill. But I wouldn't worry about it too much. You probably made enough noise thrashing around out here to scare any off."

He dropped to one knee in the clearing he'd made and rested his arms on the other bent knee. He reminded me of football players on the sidelines during a game.

"You know, preacher," he said, "I've been going over some things in my mind that we talked about earlier, and I've got another question for you."

"I don't suppose there's any way I can keep you from asking it, is there?"

I didn't know what was coming, but I was starting to lose a little patience with him, even though my subconscious mind had now convinced me that his goading was simply a way of motivating me or maybe leading me to some answers. Almost like a law professor engaged in the Socratic method in a law school class. I'd never been in a law school class, but at least it was sorta how I envisioned it.

My conscious mind, though, told me that Socrates and his method had nothing to do with it. Gabe was just being a jerk. After all, drawing on the law school analogy, there seemed to be precedent for that conclusion.

"Okay, so here's my question," Gabe said.

"I knew it."

"Now, hear me out, preacher. Hear me out. Besides, what else have you got to do?"

"I could be crawling for help."

"Yeah, that seems to be a good use of your time. You've really covered a lot of ground. I'd hate to stop you from picking up another first down."

"Okay, fine."

He stood, walked over, and sat on a nearby tree stump and folded his arms across his chest. Same cocky grin. Some might even call it a smirk. I would.

"A little while ago, back over there by the plane—and, gee, congratulations on the whole couple of first downs you've gained since you left it—you got kinda testy when you thought

I was suggesting that you should stay with the plane. Remember that? Wasn't that a hoot? First, you said you thought you should stay by the plane but then, when I agreed, you got your nose all twisted out of joint."

How could I forget? And that crack about the nose hit home. I'd broken it at least twice in my life, thanks to my football career and an automobile accident, but I didn't think that was what he meant. So I stayed quiet, not wanting to give him the satisfaction of knowing how irritated I was. I was afraid it would just encourage him.

"You made a point of telling me that you don't ever quit," he said. "I believe the way you put it was 'I never quit.'"

"I said that. And I meant it. And while we're handing out congratulations, kudos to you for being able to interpret 'I never quit' as meaning I don't ever quit. What a keen mind you have."

He lowered his head in a mock bow. "Yeah, I'm quick like that. My question, though, is where did that come from? That 'I don't quit . . . I never quit' bravado. You told me one time how you quit going to church when you were a teenager and then how you quit football at SMU and then you even quit school there altogether. Seems like you've got a pretty long history of quitting. But now, you make 'quit' sound like a four-letter word."

"It is a four-letter word. I take it basic arithmetic isn't your strong suit."

That got a laugh out of him. Got one out of me, too – and it hurt. I rolled onto my side to ease the pain, then over to my back again and worked my way up against a tree trunk with my elbows. I slipped off the backpack and raised myself as close to a sitting position as I could, at least until renewed pain in my lower back stopped me. Fortunately, my legs didn't hurt. Glass half full? I even chuckled out loud at that thought. Gallows humor, I supposed, even though I was the one on the gallows.

"Well," I said, "there's a story behind that."

"I'm all ears. And besides, like I said before, what else have you got to do?"

I laughed again, then cut it off as a spasm shot down my spine. It felt like a bolt of electricity coursing through my back, but it died before it reached my legs. Still nothing there.

He must have read my grimace. "Does it hurt?" he asked.

"Only when I laugh."

We both laughed again. This laugh-fest was about to do me in. Still, it beat crying.

"I'm all ears," Gabe said.

"Okay. Well, this goes back twenty years, to 1945, the closing year of World War II."

CHAPTER SEVEN

Even though nearly a year had passed since I graduated from Fort Worth's Polytechnic High School—Go Parrots!—and was denied by my parents the opportunity to enlist in the Marines, my desire to serve my country, like so many others, including many I had gone to high school with, still stirred inside me. It was a time of high patriotism in the land, with battles raging on two fronts, in Europe and in the Pacific. It didn't seem fair that so many of my peers were overseas while I was safely at home enjoying the fruits of their sacrifice. When I first graduated, I got caught up in that prairie fire of patriotism and felt that it would be tantamount to cowardice to accept the football scholarship to SMU. The thought of playing a kid's game while my former classmates were fighting and, in some instances dying, seemed almost un-American. I suppose I might have felt differently had our nation not been at war, but it was no time for hypotheticals. The fact of the matter was that the country was at war and it needed every able-bodied man—which I construed as including able-bodied teenagers—to fight for it.

But I honored my parents' wishes and bypassed the military for college – though what choice did I really have, since I was underage? And, in hindsight, just how did that work out for me, nearly crippled by a gridiron injury? Although, I suppose, the "almost crippled" part was hyperbole, but that's how it seemed to my adolescent mind at the time.

I again honored my parents' wishes and only dropped out of SMU—or, as Gabe put it, "quit" both the football team and college—in exchange for a promise to start going to church again. Which I couldn't have done had I not "quit" going to church in the first place. I might not like the way Gabe said things and was starting to regret having told him anything personal, but maybe he simply had touched a raw nerve with his accuracy. But again, what choice did I have? I was seventeen and had no place to live except at home with my folks once I gave up my scholarship and the cramped dorm room that came with it. So, since I needed a place to live, and it was going to be under my parents' roof, I had to return to church. That didn't mean I had to like it, though.

But this time things worked out a little better than an almost crippled ankle. Not only did I find a place for myself at Polytechnic Baptist Church in the music program, led by Dallas Alford, I started singing in a men's quartet. I even met a girl I liked. A raven-haired beauty with a slightly pug nose, twinkling eyes, and a love of laughter, which made her a good audience for my sophomoric attempts at humor. Her name was Juanita Peacock and she was part of that music program, as well. She sang as part of a women's sextet with her lovely alto voice. I actually already knew who she was because I knew some of her brothers from Poly High. In fact, one of them, Kenny, played in the same backfield as I did, earning all-district honors while I was honorable mention.

I couldn't really see a future for myself with her at first, though. To me she was just the older sister of one of my buddies. Looking back on it, I supposed more realistically it was a matter of her being unable to see a future for herself with me.

Semantics.

Still, she was awfully nice to look at and to be around.

As the war dragged on into 1945, even though it showed some promise of ending, at least in Europe, two of my closest friends from Poly decided to join the U.S. Army in April. They urged me to sign up with them. It wasn't the Marines, like I initially wanted to join, but there was courage in numbers. Plus, we had the foolish bravado of youth motivating us, coupled with an irrational fear that the war would end before we got a chance to get our licks in. This time, I was able to prevail upon my parents and obtain their permission—I guess they figured I was close enough to 18 that there was no point in resisting—so I signed up along with my two buddies. And just like that, and with very little rational thought, I became a soldier in the United States Army.

If I was being perfectly honest with myself, I'd have to admit I had an ulterior motive for joining the army, besides patriotism. My feelings for Juanita were morphing from the initial "brotherly/sisterly love" kind of relationship we had established at first, to admiration then on to infatuation on my part. Pretty soon, I was experiencing something more. Something much more. Something deeper. Something impossible.

The problem was that I knew she had stalled out at the brotherly-sisterly love stage, and she still thought of me more as a younger brother, one of her own brothers' buddies. But I realized something else was brewing inside me that didn't fit that paradigm, something that could never be. It seemed preposterous, even to me, that there could ever be anything serious between us, so I tried to hide my feelings. That was starting to become an uphill struggle so, when my buddies announced they were off to sign up for the military, I figured the best way for me to *get over* Juanita was to *get away* from Juanita.

Or, as Gabe might put it, to "quit" Juanita. Fortunately I hadn't told him about that.

So, I prevailed on my parents to okay my decision to enter the service—I'm sure they had no idea that Juanita played any part in it—and, although I was still a few months shy of eighteen, they relented and I became a part of the United States Army.

By then, the war in Europe was virtually over, though it wouldn't officially end until the Germans unconditionally surrendered on May 8. The war in the Pacific was still raging, though, and I wanted to get my licks in against a hated enemy while I still could. Watch out, Japan, another Poly Parrot was on his way.

My buddies and I were shipped off to Fort Sam Houston, near San Antonio, for induction. Then they were sent to

California for basic training, while I, as the sole remaining Parrot of our little threesome, was designated to do basic at Camp Hood, which later became a permanent installation in 1950 and its name was changed to Fort Hood. So there I was without my buddies, whose synergy I had relied on to sign up in the first place. Alone. And miserable.

But Camp Hood was near Killeen, Texas, which was only about 150 miles from Fort Worth, with buses running regularly between the two. Before long, I found myself going home every available weekend, ostensibly to see my family, but I sure spent a lot of time at the Peacock hacienda. And the more I visited, the more certain I began to feel about my love for Juanita. The problem was that I still knew it couldn't possibly be reciprocated. That led to another decision I made after basic training.

But the point of this particular story isn't about Juanita and my relationship with her. Instead, it's about an incident that happened at Camp Hood on the first full day of basic training. That was when I, along with the rest of the new guys, was introduced to a drill instructor, a DI, who seemed to me to be the epitome of evil. I had had some tough football coaches in my day, playing for Luther Scarborough at Poly High and Jimmy Stewart (no, not Jimmy Stewart the actor) during my abbreviated stint at SMU. Ironically, I was at SMU because my parents wouldn't let me enlist in the military, while Stewart was the interim head coach at SMU because the regular coach, Matty Bell, was serving in the United States Navy.

The DI wasn't very tall, a couple of inches shorter than my own five feet nine inches, but he manifested a persona that well exceeded six feet. He was wiry of build, but there was no disguising that beneath his skin lay a finely-toned, well-muscled foundation that was likely the culmination of years of physical training. A banty rooster, full of swagger despite his short stature, he would haunt my dreams both during basic training and even thereafter.

We learned early on that DIs loved push-ups, the All-American exercise, but ours refined it to an art form. Over the course of basic training, I think the most common words out of his mouth, other than a remarkable reservoir of curse words often used together in some of the most creative combinations I had ever heard, were "Drop and give me twenty-five." Nobody had to ask, "Twenty-five what?" Push-ups, of course. We quickly learned that we couldn't win with him. The system was rigged.

Case in point.

One time he stopped in front of a recruit who seemed to be lagging while doing calisthenics. The DI parked himself in front of this poor recruit and, after a torrent of blue language wilted the guy, he bellowed, "Lift your left leg."

The recruit lifted his left leg.

"Lift your right leg," he bellowed.

The recruit put his left leg down and lifted his right.

The DI got right in his face, inches away. Nose to nose. "Who told you to put your left leg down? Drop and give me twenty-five."

Man, you just couldn't win. It almost got to the point that if the DI ever singled any of us out for anything, or even stopped in front of us while we were in formation, we figured we might as well drop and start doing push-ups even before being told.

On the first full day of training, early in the morning, before the sun was fully up, we assembled on the parade ground in front of a raised platform. The DI stood on the platform wearing army-issue olive green pants and boots and a tee-shirt that hugged his torso. He informed us that we were going to start the day with calisthenics. And so we did.

We started with what some called "jumping jacks," also known as the "side straddle hop." In this exercise, we started by standing at attention then, on his command, we jumped and landed on the soles of our feet with our legs spread while swinging our arms overhead to clap above us, then jumped again to our starting position, arms back at our sides.

Sounds simple enough. And it was, for the first hundred or so. I don't know how many jumping jacks we did that first day, but it had to have been in the multiple hundreds. By the time we finished, I could barely raise my arms, much less clap them over my head. And you could forget about any more jumping. My legs had turned to rubber.

Then the DI said, "Assume the leaning rest position."

Better known as the "up" position for push-ups. I got down and assumed the position, with arms that felt like limp noodles and legs wobbling beneath me. But at least I could feel them.

Then we proceeded to do push-ups, on his count.

"Down–"

We all went down.

"Up–"

We all came up.

"Down–"

We all went down.

"Up–"

But then the tempo picked up. It went from "Down . . . up . . . down . . . up . . . down . . . up" to "down . . up . . down . . up" to "down up down up."

It was like a train starting up and pulling away, picking up speed. Pretty soon it had left the station and was headed out across the countryside. "Downupdownupdownupdownup."

I couldn't help but notice in my peripheral vision that it seemed like fewer and fewer men made it to "up" after a "down." I was determined not to be one of those that failed to get off the ground, but the inevitable ultimately happened. We did push-ups until every last man among us had completely given out and lay sprawled on the grass. Some crying like babies. Others vomiting into the grass. Some simply lying face down, not moving.

It was a little hard to complain, though, because for every jumping jack we had done earlier, the DI did one, too, up on that platform. When we assumed the "leaning rest" position—and I won't go into the absurdity of calling this "rest"—he did, too. Every time he said "down," he went down. And every time he said "up," he went up. As the train picked up speed, he also picked up speed. Downupdownupdownupdownup.

When we had all given out and groveled in the dirt, he continued to count and continued to go down and up and down and up and down and up, like an automaton. A machine. By the end of that exercise, he left us no doubt who was the best man among us.

When we finished calisthenics, or maybe it was when the calisthenics finished us, we were directed to a stack of backpacks, or rucksacks, by the barracks, that had been loaded, or lined, with something heavy. I never looked inside to see if it was sandbags or weights or exactly what, but mine felt as if it must have weighed 50 pounds as I struggled to put it on. I suspect that was a pretty accurate guess.

Once we had the rucks strapped on, which caused all of us to sag under the weight, in danger of being pulled over onto our backs unless we crouched forward to compensate, we started out for what began as a march but turned into a run alternating with a march. As we moved across the central Texas countryside, the DI marched and ran along with us. Well, not exactly with us. Instead, he literally ran circles around our tightly-packed group, cursing and berating us at every step. Soon the tightly-packed group began to stretch out. As stragglers dropped off, he'd search them out and get in their faces, screaming until they were back on their feet and moving, even if uncomfortably behind us.

By the time we returned to the parade ground by our barracks, we had probably covered at least 10 miles, maybe more. Back in the relative safety of "home," we were permitted to take off our rucks and were ordered to assemble in formation.

Then we had to wait, standing at attention in the hot Texas sun as the last few stragglers filtered in. All the while, the DI strutted in front of us. Silently at first.

The most obscene silence I have ever beheld. Then he spoke.

"Any of you men who want to quit, can. Just break ranks and gather over there."

He pointed to an area near the barracks.

"No questions asked. This is an all-volunteer army, so if this isn't for you, just huddle up over there and we'll muster you out."

There was silence and stillness for a brief moment as we all wondered whether he was serious. When we finally figured out he was for real, then *wham!* Men rushed past me to the mustering area, nearly knocking me down in the process. By the time the dust settled, close to half our number had separated from the group and gathered in a huddle by the barracks. The DI walked over and paced back and forth in front of them, as they awaited instructions on how to get out and get home.

After a few rotations, he turned to face the group of us who remained. I'll never forget his words.

"Look at them," he said. "Just look at them."

We did. I noticed that none of them would make eye contact back with any of us. Every gaze was directed at the ground, as they all seemed to know what was coming.

"They're quitters," he said. Something about the way he said the word made it sound like the most profane word I had ever heard. "We've got boys dying overseas, and they're *quitters*."

He paused and looked at the thoroughly-chastened group, then directed his attention back to those of us who remained. "And the truth is, some of you ought to be over there with them. You simply didn't have the guts to quit. You're no better than they are."

He stared at each one of us, one at a time, until he had made eye contact with every man.

"Fall out."

"Things might have been different before, but ever since then, quitting just isn't in my vocabulary," I said, "even though it might make the most sense, sometimes. I can still hear that DI's voice in my head every time I think about quitting something I've started. So, like I told you: I don't quit."

Gabe had sat silently and listened as I talked. When I finished, he nodded. "Well, then, I guess you better get going."

I rolled over onto my stomach and began inching my way forward again.

CHAPTER EIGHT

Notwithstanding the pride I felt in my seemingly unbreakable watch, checking the time as I crawled didn't seem important so, again, I wasn't sure how many hours I had been at it. I could tell by the position of the sun above the treetops that it must have been afternoon on Wednesday. I stopped and rolled onto my back, using the backpack to prop up my head. I checked my watch – still ticking. Sure enough, it was shortly before two o'clock. Surely, we had been missed by now.

Our original schedule was to fly out Wednesday morning around nine or ten o'clock, which should have put us back at Red Bird Airport by noon at the latest. From there, after hangaring the plane, it was only about a ten or fifteen minute drive home to Duncanville. Juanita might not have thought much of an hour delay, but surely approaching two hours would have set her in motion.

It would only take a call to the Evangelism Division to check on me, which likely would have led to a call to Evadale to check on our departure. Word that we had left the night before would surely set alarm bells to ringing. That would have led to a search being organized and . . . well, then the searchers would have needed to figure out where in about 560,000 acres, or nearly 900 square miles, a tiny four-seater single engine plane might have set down. That was a tall order.

Still, having searchers spreading out over that much land was better than having no searchers at all.

And maybe I could make it easier for them if I could just get to that highway. All day, I heard sporadic sounds of traffic. It wasn't a well-traveled highway, obviously, but it was traveled, nonetheless. That meant possible rescue was at least within earshot.

Of course, I couldn't see anything through the denseness of the trees. There could have been a highway a quarter mile off and I wouldn't have seen anything, even if I had been on foot. To make matters worse, my point of view from ground level was more limited than if I had been able to stand, or on my hands and knees. But I refused to allow myself to get discouraged. I couldn't let dwelling on what I was unable to do stop me; I had to dwell on what I was able to do. And that was to crawl.

I realized quickly that I was going to have to recalculate how long it would take me to cover a mile because of the logistics of my path. There were plenty of fallen trees in the forest and, when I confronted one, I was unable to climb over it. Not just big trees, but any trees. Instead, I was forced to snake my way along the length of the tree until I reached one end or the other, then I could crawl around to the other side and continue my journey forward.

It was interesting what priorities you developed in a situation like that. As I traversed the floor of the Big Thicket, it occurred to me that my idea of luxury had been reduced from a fancy resort hotel to simply lying on something soft with a blanket I could pull over me to keep warm, an aspirin, a glass of water, and a cup of ice. Thirst was becoming a real factor. Since I had finished the dregs of coffee in the thermos, I'd had nothing to drink for going on twelve or fifteen hours. I wasn't hungry, to my surprise, but I was parched to the extent that the thought of water became an obsession almost as much as reaching that highway.

At one point, just before arriving at my current resting spot, I reached a stump about two feet tall, where a tree had broken off and fallen. I crawled right up the stump, reached in, and felt a tiny bit of moisture. I couldn't raise myself high enough off the ground to get my face into the stump to drink. I looked around and found a nice, full leaf. Carefully, I lifted it into the stump and forced it under the small bit of water. Then I brought it back out, put it in my mouth, and sucked the tiny bit of moisture that clung to it. I repeated the process until there was no moisture left in the stump.

It wasn't much, but it sure was nice. I thought back to my childhood days, in the summers in Fort Worth. I remembered following along, with my buddies, behind the ice wagon as it made its deliveries. We picked up tiny slivers of ice that fell onto the street from the wagon and sucked on them like popsicles. That memory made me realize how jaded kids were today, with soft drinks and icees and slurpees and fruit drinks, to the point that they had no idea just how good a single sliver of ice on a 100 degree Texas day could be. Context was everything.

I ended my break and rolled onto my chest and began again, digging in with my elbows and pulling my way forward. After a few minutes, I spotted a small clearing in the midst of a thick stand of trees up ahead. It looked to me as if it had been deliberately cleared, maybe as a campsite. Boy Scouts, probably.

I dug deep with my elbows and pulled forward, inching along at a snail's pace. As I drew closer, I saw a figure in the clearing, squatting with his hands out, as if warming them over a campfire. A brief moment of optimism flared. Then I realized who it was.

Gabe.

He turned and looked my way. "Come on, preacher, you can do it," he said. He stood and clapped his hands. "Come on, boy," he said, as if calling to a dog.

It seemed as if it took an hour, though it was more likely fifteen minutes, but at last I pulled myself into the clearing where he waited. Sure enough, the remnants of what looked like a fairly recent fire filled a depression in the middle of the clearing. Charred wood, but not smoking wood. Still, as recent as perhaps a few days or so prior. That meant it wasn't unheard of for people to visit this part of the Thicket.

I rolled onto my back, again using the backpack as a pillow. Gabe resumed his squatting position and nodded.

"You know, too bad we burned all your sermon notes," he said. "Wouldn't a fire here be nice?"

All I could do was nod. I felt exhausted, every feeling part of my body ached, and I didn't think I could move again for hours. Even if I had to.

"What, no smart aleck comment?" he asked.

"I'm just wondering why you keep hanging around."

"It's boring being dead, and you're the only show around."

"I'm glad I can amuse you."

Gabe stood and walked the circumference of the clearing. "So, what do you suppose this is? Some kind of campsite?"

"Boy Scouts, maybe?"

"As good a guess as any, I suppose." He stopped next to a fallen tree on the outer perimeter. Squatted again and looked at the ground along the tree's length.

"This is interesting," he said. "Looks like someone dug a hole here at one time."

I rolled onto my side and propped myself up on an elbow. "What do you mean?"

Gabe pointed at the ground. "It's kinda sunken here, like a depression in the ground. Like it was once a hole but has since been filled in."

I swung back into action, exhaustion now a memory. In my own inimitable style, I elbowed my way across the clearing until I reached the spot where Gabe stood. Sure enough, there was a depression running the length of the tree, about fifteen feet or so, toward the upturned root ball. It gave the appearance of having been loosely covered with dirt to hide a hole. But why would anyone dig a hole here?

"Latrine?" Gabe asked.

I pulled my head back suddenly. Not what I was thinking, but also not what I wanted to think.

"Buried body?" he asked.

Again, not one of my favored options. I sniffed the dirt.

"Smells like water," I said.

"You're kidding, right? You can smell water in dirt?"

"You know what I'm talking about. Like the smell of fresh rain or when you've watered your lawn. I'm betting this used to be a water hole."

"You've got some imagination, preacher."

I looked toward the root ball. There, as clear as day, I saw what looked like a splash of paint on the base of the fallen tree, and an even deeper depression that had been exposed by the uprooted trunk.

"There," I said, pointing at it. "See the paint? I've heard that Indians used to mark springs by splashing paint on rocks and trees nearby."

"Like I said, you've got some imagination, preacher. Are you trying to tell me you think some Indians—whatever tribes used to be in these parts—found a spring here and marked it just for you to find?"

"Alabama and Coushatta."

"Beg pardon?"

"Those were the two major tribes that inhabited this area. And they sure wouldn't have marked a spring for someone in the future to find, but they might have for themselves to find."

"Just how long ago was this? Don't you think that even if this had been a spring once, it's probably dried up by now?"

"There's one way to find out."

I inched my way to the root, to the deeper indentation where the paint mark was. I began clawing at the dirt, pulling up handfuls and tossing it aside. Little by little, I deepened the depression into a hole.

Gabe leaned over me from behind. He began speaking, softly at first, but increasingly louder until he sounded like a drill instructor screaming in my ear. In fact, I could hear the voice of my old DI from Camp Hood as Gabe chanted.

"Dig, preacher, dig. Dig. Dig. Dig dig dig dig dig! Get dirty! Dig that hole."

I realized that the dirt had turned into a clay-like substance.

I looked at my hands and realized it was mud.

Mud! That meant there was water down there somewhere.

I kept clawing and throwing the handfuls aside. When I had dug as far as I could reach, my whole arm beneath the level of the ground, I felt moisture. Not much, but some. No longer mud, but a wet, squishy sandy loam.

I pulled my handkerchief from my suit coat pocket, draped it over my hand, then reached down and scooped out a handful of that loam. I tied the handkerchief around it, then twisted the knot. I held it above my upturned head, mouth open, and squeezed for all I was worth. A drop of moisture emerged and dangling tantalizingly over my mouth.

Then fell into it.

Another drop. Another fall. Again and again, one drop at a time, until there was no more to give.

I felt as if I had just downed a gallon of iced tea. It soothed and moistened my chapped mouth and lips, then rolled down my throat.

I looked up at Gabe and smiled.

He stood there for a moment, then began clapping his hands. Slowly at first then faster.

"Good job, preacher man. Good job."

CHAPTER NINE

Juanita Farris sat at the kitchen table of her tidy home in Duncanville. It was nothing fancy, certainly not a mansion, but it was comfortable and had become home in the short time they had been living there. Three bedrooms, one in the middle of a hallway that Corky Bo and Stevie shared, sleeping on bunk beds, a second for Darlyne at one end of the hall and the master bedroom at the opposite end from Darlyne. Calling it a "master" was generous, but at least it had its own bathroom and tiny shower, while the kids were relegated to sharing the other bathroom across the hall from the boys' room.

It had a small living room just inside the front door, while a den and kitchen flowed together on the other side of the house, with a door leading to a two car garage. Comfortable. Tidy.

She sat and stared at the clock on the wall, not moving since hanging up the phone. The hands showed the time to be 3:45. It had been an hour since that call, and she felt an overwhelming sense of panic building inside. She needed to keep it together, though, when the older kids got home, which should be any time now.

Darlyne, at eleven years old, was in the sixth grade, which was the first year at Duncanville Junior High School. Mary McCombs, wife of the pastor at First Baptist Church, had graciously offered to pick her up after school today so Juanita could stay by the phone. Corky Bo, at nine, was in the fourth grade at Merrifield Elementary School, not that far from where they lived, so he would be walking home. Stevie, the youngest at four years old, was playing with his toy cars in the den. She could hear their tiny wheels spinning on the linolcum floor.

Juanita and Corky had lived in Duncanville for only a

few months, transferring there from Wrightstown, New Jersey. They had moved to Wrightstown while on furlough from the mission field in Japan, so that Corky could pastor a church there while studying at Johns Hopkins University in Baltimore.

Corky had received an unexpected call from the Evangelism Division of the Baptist General Convention of Texas with an offer for him to join the division as an evangelist. They both had anticipated that the family would be returning to Japan to continue their missionary work after his furlough ended. But, after much prayerful consideration, Corky tendered his resignation to the Southern Baptist Convention's Foreign Mission Board and they returned to Texas, a scant thirty miles from where they had each grown up in east Fort Worth.

Because the decision was made on short notice, they hadn't had a chance to scout out a house in Dallas, but Corky's friend Gabriel Rogers was a building contractor who not only lived in Duncanville, he also built houses in the town. He offered to rent them one of his homes that was unoccupied until they had a chance to look around. Or, if they liked the house he rented them at 201 Azalea Lane, they could continue to live there. It was extremely convenient, only about a fifteen or twenty minute drive from the Evangelism Division's offices in downtown Dallas, so they accepted the offer and moved in.

Living in Duncanville offered them a chance at a far more normal life than they'd been accustomed to in Japan. Well, for that matter since they had been married in 1947. Their lives revolved around school for the first decade of their marriage, with both of them attending classes at Baylor and again at New Orleans Baptist Theological Seminary.

Then Juanita dropped out of school in 1953 for the birth of their first child, Darlyne. Their second child, Mike, was born two years later, while Corky continued his studies at the seminary, culminating with a Doctorate in Theology. There had been some logistical difficulties during the seminary years, when Corky was asked to serve as pastor of the newly-founded Goodwood Baptist Church in Baton Rouge while still attending classes in New Orleans. They had found a place to live in Baton Rouge, but Corky lived in campus housing during the weekdays, so they were really together only on weekends.

Then came the move to Japan, first to Tokyo and then to Sapporo, on the northern island of Hokkaido, so life again revolved around school—this time language school in Tokyo, where both of them studied Japanese—and church, with their missionary responsibilities. Things were a bit easier in Tokyo because they lived in a compound of homes occupied by American families, mostly missionary, so there were friendly faces and an easily understood language, and kids for theirs to play with.

Juanita had worried a bit at first after the move to Japan. She feared they would be depriving their children of normal lives, but both of them thrived not only in the compound in Tokyo, but also in school. Darlyne attended American School in Japan while in Tokyo, then both she and Corky Bo were enrolled in Hokkaido International School once the family moved to the northern island.

But as much as Juanita loved Japan, she had to admit she was happy when the Lord called them to return to her native state, where she could once again be close to her family in Fort Worth. Things really seemed to settle down after the move. They joined First Baptist Church in Duncanville, and the kids made good friends there with whom they also went to school. Corky was home during the weeks, although sometimes he was gone on weekends, typically driving to one location or another around Texas to fill in for pastors in local church pulpits when those pastors were on vacation. He also had to travel longer distances on occasion for work-related meetings, but rarely overnight.

She hadn't thought much about it when Corky and Gabe flew to the Texas panhandle a couple of days earlier, because she knew it was quicker and easier, and most likely safer, than crossing the state by car on such a tight schedule. She knew flying would bring him home sooner. But he should have been home hours ago.

When she had called his office at the Evangelism Division, no one had heard from him, nor did they even expect to. According to one of his colleagues, Byron Richardson, Corky had told him that he and Gabe would be spending last night in southeast Texas and flying back to the Dallas area this morning. He hadn't given a definite take-off time, but said it would be after breakfast, so probably mid-morning. Byron said Corky also told him he would then be going straight home rather than to the office first, since he had been gone for two days and the Red Bird Airport, where they would be landing, was just minutes from Duncanville.

She wasn't too worried when he hadn't gotten home by noon, knowing that the departure time was most likely flexible. And by one or two, well, she figured he had gone to the office anyway, probably to follow up on the meetings he had been in the past two days. It was a little out of character for him not to have called, but she didn't put too much stock in that.

She called Gabe's wife around 2:30, who told her Gabe hadn't gotten home yet, either, though she wasn't worried. She figured he had gone to check some of the construction sites his company was building since he had been gone for a couple of days. No, she hadn't heard from him, but that wasn't too unusual. She figured he'd be home when he got home.

But at 2:45, when she called Byron again and he still had not seen or heard from Corky, Juanita began to seriously worry. Then she had gotten that call back from Byron a half hour ago.

"Juanita," he said, "I talked to the folks from last night's meeting in southeast Texas, and they said Corky and Gabe left last night."

She felt as if someone had dripped ice water down her spine. "Are you sure?"

"The pastor said one of his deacons drove them to the air strip and they took off. That was about ten or so last night."

"He's sure they took off? Couldn't they have changed their minds and gone to a hotel?"

"The deacon said he watched them then he turned off the lights at the landing strip and drove home. Even if they had turned around, they couldn't have landed. And they wouldn't have had a car there, anyway."

"Then why didn't they get home last night? Surely a ten o'clock take-off would have put them back here by midnight at the latest."

"They're trying to figure it out now. Like I said, the word I got is that the plane took off around ten p.m., and no one's heard from them since. The pastor said he would call the sheriff's department and let me know if there was any news."

Tears filled Juanita's eyes and dread filled her heart. She hadn't felt this way since Stevie's health problems that had necessitated an emergency trip from Japan to Texas a few years ago. Ten o'clock last night, and no word? Where could he be? She had just been sitting there at the kitchen table ever since, waiting for that next phone call. The call she was dreading.

As she thought back over their nearly eighteen-year marriage, she couldn't help but wonder if this was the end. Then she dismissed the thought as soon as it crossed her mind. Surely not. She and Corky had always shared a connection, often thinking and feeling the same things without having to speak. Sometimes she was able to anticipate his thoughts and feelings, even his actions. Often, she even knew before he did what he was going to do. If he was gone, she would know it. No, he was still alive. This was not the end. He was out there somewhere. She just had to find him.

CHAPTER TEN

"So, you've told me how you met your buddy's sister Juanita at church," Gabe said.

I lay on my side, resting and gearing up for another spurt of crawling. Gabe sat cross-legged on the ground, his back against a large tree trunk, watching me.

"You said neither one of you really saw any future in it," he continued, "but that obviously changed."

"Obviously."

"I've heard of guys running off to join the French Foreign Legion to get over a girl, but I guess I never really thought about joining the U.S. Army. That's not nearly as far away. Unless there's a war going on."

"And there was."

"So how'd it happen if you were off in the service? The two of you getting together, I mean."

"Well, I guess I knew a lot earlier than Juanita did that there might be more between us. The trick would be to get her to see it before the army could send me to the other side of the world. I wasn't even real sure, at the time, if it would be possible to change her mind. So I really thought maybe the best thing was to go and try to forget about her."

After completing basic training, I expected to be sent overseas but the army surprised me and assigned me permanently to Camp Hood. "Permanently" was military-speak that didn't really mean permanently, but only meant for the duration of my enlistment. Though I was just on the verge of turning eighteen, I knew I was in love with Juanita, notwithstanding our six-year age difference, and that she was who God intended me to marry. In hindsight, that all seems rather silly, especially since we hadn't really had what you could call a "date," just group get-togethers with kids from church. Still, I knew what I knew. It was too bad she didn't know what I knew.

Besides, she already had a boyfriend, some guy in the Coast Guard, if you can believe that. So, to protect my mental state and forestall frustration on that front, I asked for reassignment overseas. The army agreed to my request, telling me to bone up on Japan because I'd be spending some time there. That was more than 6,000 miles from Fort Worth, so I wouldn't be making any weekend trips home like I could from Camp Hood, which was only about 150 miles away. That was fine with me. I figured the farther away from Juanita I was, the better for my emotional health. Then maybe I could convince myself that I hadn't lost out to the Coast Guard; I had simply lost out to distance. It was amazing what you could convince yourself of if you really put your mind to it.

But there was no "quit" in me, not after it had been driven out of me in basic training. So, when the army told me that it was mandatory that I take a two-week furlough before going overseas—the idea was that one last trip home might ease the homesickness for soldiers heading overseas; bad idea!—I decided to take advantage of that one last opportunity. If I couldn't make it work this time, I would write off any hope of a relationship with Juanita, but I owed it to myself to make one last effort.

It was good to be back home in Fort Worth, even if only for a couple of weeks. Both my brothers were married and out of the house, but Mom and Dad made sure I didn't feel lonesome. And I spent as much time as I could with Juanita. It was usually with church friends, so we were all together in a group, or at her house, under the guise of visiting her brothers, my old teammates from Poly. The trick was trying to find an opportunity in private, without her brothers or the others from the church group around, to press my case with her before shipping out. I found that to be as frustrating as anything I had ever done. Even when I thought I might get some one-on-one time with her, Kenny or one of her other brothers would pop in at the most inopportune time.

Finally, one evening shortly before I was to return to camp to ship out, I managed to get her alone on the front porch of her house. I don't remember how I managed to work it, getting her out there alone, but there we were, sitting on a porch swing and sipping lemonade on a hot Texas summer night. I had practiced, in my head, what I was going to say but every time I started to speak, my nerves shut down my mouth.

I'm sure it must have seemed awkward to her, sitting alone with her "younger brother," and I hoped I could get up enough courage to say something before we were interrupted. Fortunately, she got the ball rolling.

"You seem awful quiet," she said.

"I guess I'm just a little nervous about what's next."

"You mean in Japan?"

"Yeah. I've never been anywhere outside of Texas."

"I'm just glad the war is nearly over, so I hope you'll be safe."

I nodded, gulped some lemonade, and got quiet again.

"Is that all that's bothering you?" she asked.

"Just a little worried about being away from everybody."

"You'll make friends. You're good at that."

"And I'll miss Mom and Dad. And Buddy and Webber." My brothers.

More lemonade, then I squeezed up all the courage I could muster. "And you."

"That's sweet. I'll miss you, too."

I nodded and my throat went dry. More lemonade.

"I wonder about what's going to happen with us," I said.

"I promise I'll write, if you will, too," she said. She nudged me on the shoulder with hers. "After all, you're my favorite brother."

"What if I don't want to just be your favorite brother?"

She twisted around in the swing so that she was half-facing me. I could tell that she was trying to read my face, which I hoped was a blank slate but also kind of hoped was telling her the meaning behind my words.

The latter prevailed, and her expression fell as she realized what I meant.

"There is no 'us,' Corky," she said. "You know that as well as I do."

"Maybe. I don't know." I shrugged and looked down at the nearly empty lemonade glass I was holding.

She shifted again in the swing so she now faced me head on. Her face reflected the seriousness with which she spoke.

"I'm six years older than you. Most girls I grew up with are already married or at least engaged to be married. And now you're getting ready to go overseas for a year. I can't just put my life on hold and wait for you."

I felt a faint glimmer of hope in my heart. She hadn't said she didn't love me. She didn't even bring up ol' Coast Guard. All she did was point out practicalities, like our age difference. But practicalities could be overcome. The age difference might seem big now, but when she was sixty and I was fifty-four, would it really matter? And she was the one who said the M word, not me. Did that mean she was already thinking about it?

"Besides, what about Cliff?" she asked.

Oh, yeah. Ol' Coast Guard. So she brought him up after all. And he was more than just a practicality.

"Are y'all engaged?" I asked.

"No."

"Have you even talked about getting married?"

"Well, no. But that's beside the point."

"Do you love him?"

She had no answer for that. Not even "none of your business," which she would certainly have been justified in saying to her impertinent "favorite brother."

I pressed my advantage. "Does he love you?" I paused, then added, "As much as I do?" That last part slipped out before I could stop it. I held my breath and waited.

Again, no answer.

I could tell three things by her non-answer and her expression, though. One, she didn't love him. Two, he hadn't told her he loved her. And three, she was shocked to hear me say that I loved her. All this time, she had thought we were just friends, all part of a big group of young people, or one of her brothers' football buddies, but now she was seeing me in a different light.

"Look, Corky, you're a great guy," she said. I braced myself for the bad news to follow. "You're a great guy" is nearly always followed by "but."

Sure enough.

"But it could never work out. By the time you get back from Japan, you'll have forgotten about me."

"I won't forget."

"You say that now, but you will. You know you will."

But I knew I wouldn't.

I left her house that evening satisfied that I had done all I could do. I had surprised even myself by speaking out so boldly, but at least now, she knew how I felt. I wouldn't have to live with the aftermath of a failure to speak. Still, there wasn't much I could do about it at that point. Maybe she would think about what I'd said and change her mind; maybe she wouldn't. Only time would tell.

I returned to Camp Hood after the end of my furlough, but before actually shipping out to Japan, I was assigned to

Fort Oglethorpe, Georgia, to the Adjutant General's School. I was to spend six weeks in administrative training there before shipping to Yokohama, Japan. I didn't hear from her for over a month and, at that point, I hoped to fulfill Juanita's prophecy and forget about her. That's why I requested to be sent overseas in the first place. I figured if things moved forward with her and ol' Coast Guard, it would hurt less that way.

Then I received a letter from her one fateful day shortly before I was scheduled to leave. Short but, as the cliché goes, sweet.

Really sweet.

Dear Corky,

I've been giving a lot of thought to our conversation and also devoting a lot of prayer to it. My mind tells me it can never work for us, but my heart is starting to tell me different. More importantly, God is telling me different. Cliff and I broke up, and I eagerly await your return from Japan.

I love you, too.

Juanita.

Score: Army 1, Coast Guard 0

On my way to Japan from Fort Oglethorpe, I passed through Fort Worth on the way to the west coast for my ship out. That allowed me one last visit to the Peacock house, to confirm what she said in the letter. It was a brief visit, but just long enough to ask Juanita the right question, get the right answer, and buy the right ring for the right finger of her left hand. The only bad part was that now I was actually heading overseas, as I had requested, for a tour of duty that I no longer wanted. Irony is a strange and wondrous thing.

CHAPTER ELEVEN

As Juanita sat at the kitchen table and waited for the next call, she thought back to the beginning. Back to when she was just "Juanita," before "Corky and Juanita."

Although she had been raised Methodist, attending church at Polytechnic Methodist Church in east Fort Worth with her family, most of her friends she had gone to school with, and with whom she stayed close after graduation, attended Polytechnic Baptist. So she started splitting her time: Sunday school at the Methodist church and worship services at the Baptist Church. She loved singing, had a smooth alto voice, joined the Baptist choir, and became a member of a girl's ensemble there. She enjoyed that most of all.

Between working as a stenographer and bookkeeper at a car dealership, Mastin Motor Company in Fort Worth, and extracurricular activities at both churches, she didn't have a lot of time for dating, but that was fine at the time. She hadn't yet met anyone that she felt merited serious attention, so she was content with group activities.

When a new choir director, Dallas Alford – the man they joked had been so-named because of his parents' preference for Fort Worth's rival city – came to Poly Baptist, he began working directly with the young people at the church. In addition to leading the choir and the ensemble, he organized men's and women's trios, quartets, and sextets. It was at Poly Baptist, and through its music program, that she first met Corky in early 1945. She had heard of him, of course, through her brothers, who played football at Poly High. She had seen him play during his senior year, when he was in the backfield with her brother Kenny.

She had always been taken by his jet black hair, with a natural curl, which he wore stylishly long. He always seemed to have a smile on his face, beneath a slightly crooked nose, the result of performing on the gridiron in the days before facemasks on helmets. She had even seen him perform in the operetta at the high school that year. She still remembered the first time she heard his clear, smooth tenor voice. Even today, she loved to hear him sing.

Even though she and Corky got to know each other pretty well through the church music program, particularly when he became part of a men's quartet while she sang with a women's sextet, she never dreamed that anything would come of it. After all, he was younger than she was, by nearly six years, and she still thought of him more as her brothers' friend than as part of her own social group.

But over the course of the next few months, she and Corky got closer through their church activities. In fact, his mother, Mable, was her Sunday school teacher, and working with her on some Sunday school projects gave Juanita many occasions to see Corky outside of church, usually at the Farris house. From that, she began to see him more in his own merit, instead of as a friend of her brothers but, still, in her mind, she felt more like a sister to him rather than anything else.

That is, until the Spring of 1945.

The women's sextet was slated to sing one night at another of the Polytechnic neighborhood churches. Dallas Alford often arranged things like that, having one or more of his musical groups singing at other churches, trying to create a community between congregations, even those of different denominations. Juanita put on the solid red dress that was part of the group's uniform. Though modest, it still showed her petite figure and the color set off her jet black hair, a match in color so close to Corky's that it almost reinforced the brother-sister notion. She ran a brush through that hair a few last strokes, then she applied just a touch of make-up, and she was ready to go.

Juanita stepped out onto the front porch of her east Fort Worth home, where she still lived with her parents, seven younger brothers, and a baby sister. The Peacock household was packed, typically full of life, and definitely full of love. She sat in the porch swing chair to await her ride from Mary Katherine, who had been her best friend since their first year of high school. The air was faintly breezy, the temperature a comfortable eighty degrees. Winter had faded away and Spring arrived, with its promise of at least a few weeks of perfect weather before giving way to stifling 100 degree days. A typical north Texas summer.

She didn't have to wait more than a few minutes before Mary Katherine pulled to a stop out front in her dark green 1938 Ford convertible coupe. Juanita wished she had a car of her own, but dollars were tight in the overloaded Peacock household, though her income from Mastin Motor Company allowed her to contribute to the family upkeep and still provide her plenty left over for personal needs and a modest savings account.

Mary Katherine honked, even though Juanita was already sitting on the porch swing waiting.

"Did you think I wouldn't see you?" Juanita asked, laughing as she opened the passenger door and slid in. Mary Katherine wore a matching red dress.

"I was kinda hoping maybe one of your brothers would look out the window and see me," Mary Katherine said.

"Which one? Kenny? Buddy?"

"Does it matter?"

That drew peals of laughter from both of them, as Mary Katherine pulled away. Juanita tied a scarf around her hair to keep it in place. She loved riding in Mary Katherine's convertible, but it could make a mess of her hair if she wasn't careful.

"Make sure every hair's in place," Mary Katherine said, as if reading her mind. "Wouldn't want to disappoint Corky."

"Oh, hush."

"Come on and 'fess up. You like him, don't you?"

"He's nice, but he's too young for me. Besides, he and Kenny are friends."

"So what?"

"So I'm not attracted to a boy who could be my little brother."

"If you say so."

"I say so."

Mary Katherine sped up as they left the block where the Peacocks lived and pulled onto a busier street. Neither one of them saw the dark Pontiac that ran a stop sign from their right and shot into the intersection. The Ford the girls were in slammed into the driver's side of the Pontiac as it flew in front of them. There was a loud crashing noise, followed by the sound of crumpling metal.

The impact propelled Juanita forward from her seat. Her forehead hit the windshield first, then her right cheek hit. Her face flattened against the glass. Then the windshield yielded to the assault, shattering into large chunks, leaving wicked shards behind. Juanita's face pierced through as glass broke. Jagged fingers of glass tore into the side of her face.

She blacked out.

The next thing she remembered was waking up a few hours later and finding herself lying in a hospital bed. She kept her eyes closed, as if not seeing would prevent what she knew had just happened: disfigurement. How could your face pierce a windshield and not leave you disfigured? She could almost see herself now, her once beautiful face red and scarred, like a gangster in a gangster movie. Or, worse, a monster in a horror movie.

She reached for her cheek, where a stabbing pain assaulted her, but it was swathed in bandages. She knew it was simply covering up the injuries that the accident was sure to have left.

"You awake?" a male voice gently asked.

She was afraid to open her eyes, but she turned her face in

the direction of the voice.

"You really gave us a scare."

She knew the voice but wanted to see him before she believed it. She opened her eyes and blinked. Blurriness faded and her vision crystallized until she could clearly see the speaker: Corky Farris.

Was this some kind of sign? The last thing she and Mary Katherine had been talking about was him, and now he was the first thing she saw when she came to.

Maybe it was a sign.

"How long have you been here?" she asked.

"About an hour. I sent your mom and dad down to the cafeteria and said I'd watch you for a while."

"Is Mary Katherine okay?"

"The doctors said she's going to be fine."

She touched the bandages on her cheeks again. She felt tears rolling down, the salt stinging her skin. Those must have been responsible for the stabbing pain.

"I must look ugly," she said.

"Not to me. You've never looked more beautiful."

After being sent home from the hospital, Juanita spent nearly the next three weeks in bed. She had some broken bones – minor ones, in her hand and forearm – that needed to heal, not to mention bruises all over. The doctors also wanted time for the stitches on her face to do their job before she exposed it to sunlight. During that time she had a lot of visitors, but none more regular than Corky Farris. Sometimes he brought her gifts, like stuffed animals or books; sometimes he sat and talked; sometimes he just sat; and sometimes he sang to her. And sometimes she sang with him, their alto and baritone voices softly crooning hymns in a blended duet, a preview of their future.

But something else was going on in that three weeks. Ever

since they had met a few months earlier and became friends, she considered their relationship to be akin to a brother-sister kind of thing. She got the impression that he felt the same way. They talked and laughed in group outings, but it was never just the two of them. On occasion, she and other girls from the church went to his house to visit his mom, Mable – her Sunday school teacher – but even then, he was polite and friendly. Mostly from afar, though, not wanting to intrude on the class get-togethers. She knew that, without the group from church or her connection to Mable's Sunday school class, she wouldn't spend any time with him at all. On occasion, he came by to visit Kenny, but then the two of them went off somewhere together, or maybe some of her other brothers joined them, but those were more of a "hi and bye" kind of meeting.

She believed that Corky, too, thought this was merely a brother-sister thing going on. But during the three weeks he visited while she was recuperating, she began to sense that, from his end, there was starting to be something more. It was funny, but she wasn't sure if he knew that, at least not yet, but she certainly did. And maybe she was also beginning to reciprocate those feelings, though she kept it to herself. She knew it could never work, particularly given their age difference.

And so she started dating someone closer to her own age, a guy she knew from high school who had joined the Coast Guard during the war. She thought that might throw Corky off the trail, once he realized his true feelings for her – assuming he ever did. Surely the age difference and the fact that she already had a boyfriend would keep him from pursuing something more with her. That way she wouldn't have to hurt his feelings.

But after a while, once she saw that he had figured out he was in love with her, she realized that she was feeling the same way in return. So, shortly before Corky was set to ship off to Japan as part of the post-war occupation, they cleared the air: she loved him and he loved her. He asked her to marry him and, when she said yes, it seemed as if it had been inevitable from their first meeting that they would someday be together.

You might even say it was God's will.

It was odd, she thought, sitting there at the kitchen table in Duncanville nearly two decades later, how she always seemed to know things before he did. Just like she knew he loved her before he knew it, she knew before he did that he was meant to preach, and not just for a career in music. She also knew before he did that God was calling him first to the seminary, then to Japan. She even knew before he did that God was leading him back to Texas from the mission field. She sensed that he understood that she seemed to be the forerunner on those things, because he always used her as a sounding board when confronted with those decisions.

But now a worrying thought crossed her mind: Did God lead Corky back to Texas just to lose him in the dark of night? Was that God's will, too?

She wondered.

And she cried.

CHAPTER TWELVE

"Would I be safe in assuming that the army sending you to Japan had something to do with your going back as a missionary?" Gabe asked.

I lay on my back, the backpack cushioning my head. It was turning out to be more beneficial as a pillow than to hold the things I had brought with me. It seemed as if I hadn't made much progress with my crawling, but that didn't bother me. I had found that it was in times like this that it helped to think back over your life and reassess how you got to where you were, so at least my mind stayed occupied. Not that it would change my condition, but it might help me come to grips with the "why" of what had happened. If I truly believed that God had a plan for my life, then it followed that flying into treetops in the middle of a Texas winter was part of that plan—unless my own plans had subverted God's will. That would lead to a radically different conclusion, and that was the unknown I had to figure out.

"It's where it all got started," I said. "But I didn't know it at the time. The truth is, by the time I left Japan, I hoped I would never see it again."

"What changed?"

"Well, to quote a cliché, God works in mysterious ways."

By the time the army transport ship I was onboard arrived at Yokohama, a port city south of Tokyo, it was the latter part of August of 1945, and the Japanese had already surrendered, so combat operations in the Pacific had ended. I was assigned to a unit quartered there, but now as part of the occupation of Japan as opposed to an invasion. Part of me still wanted to fight, to get my licks in, but now that I knew I had a future with Juanita, my fervor for battle had cooled considerably as my likelihood of survival heated up.

I had barely gotten back on solid ground, albeit foreign soil, and already I was missing Texas. Especially Juanita. But at least now I really had something to look forward to when I returned. In the meantime, I would learn to be a correspondent, writing letters whenever I had an opportunity. With no more weekend visits to Fort Worth in the offing, the written word would have to suffice. I was glad I had told Juanita my feelings the last chance I had.

One of my treasures during this time was a letter I received from my brother Buddy, whose given name was Adrian, part of the family tradition of giving sons horrible first names: Webber, Adrian, and Theron. He was the middle child in the family, yet he was still a decade older than I. He had written the letter before the Japanese surrender on his letterhead at Sinclair Refining Company where he worked. Like so much wartime correspondence, it wasn't able to track me down for weeks and it didn't arrive until after the Japanese surrender. It said:

> *Pvt. T.V.*
>
> *Well, Corky, the time did come that we all dreaded to see although we knew it would sooner or later, so this is it. I have wanted to say a lot of things to you and just be around so we could shoot the bull more than we were able to the last few days, but things just didn't work out so we could and it's too late now, so I wrote these lines to sorta help say what I wanted to and that I really mean it.*
>
> *Son, and I say son because you seem almost as much like a son to me as a brother, you are not going to be a kid anymore when you come home again to stay and your ideas, thoughts, and habits will be a lot different than they are now, but please don't let yourself change us to lose the*

wonderful passions you have developed so quickly, that others never do in a lifetime. I mean keep that sense of humor, personality, and stay dependable and you will win any front, whether it's home or battle.

Yes, I'll admit, and want to, that we have all been mighty proud of the way you have applied and conducted yourself these few quick years and I wanted to tell you so before you left. Your leaving makes it hard for me to stay back here in the States where it's safe, even just a little longer, when I know I have everything to stay for, yet I have more to want to fight for, too.

Now, boy, I am not trying to give you advice because I'm nobody to advise anyone about anything – I only wanted to say more than just a "good by" but I knew I couldn't when the time came without puckering up a little and looking silly – besides, I'm too big to act that way now, don't you think? Ha!

So let's just let it go with a so long for now and may God stay with you.

As Ever and Always
Buddy

Over the next years, I would write regularly to Juanita, but also to Mom and Dad. I felt a little bad that I spent more of my free time writing to Juanita than to my parents, although I'm sure they understood it was largely due to those "passions" that Buddy wrote about in his letter.

Mom probably understood that better than anyone. She knew how head-over-heels I was about Juanita. A few months after I arrived in Japan, I wrote this to her, using a nickname for her that was sort of a little private joke between us – and maybe a little bit of payback for a letter I had received years earlier from my "little old nasty pipe."

Dearest Pudgy:

Hi, there, old woman. I think you're cute, though You're sure purty. Now, you're not supposed to be mad at me. For not writing any sooner, I mean. I have been awfully busy, and every time I write, I always write to Peacock first, and by the time I get through writing to her, I don't have much time to write to anyone else. That doesn't mean I don't love you, though.

I am sitting here talking to a boy from Poly right now. It is really nice to run across guys from home. I don't see many, and I was really surprised to see this ole guy up here. I hate to be an old fuddy-duddy, but I wish I were coming home, too. You know, Peacock really messed up my overseas trip. I really wanted to go before, but now I don't want to do anything but sit around and drool. No kidding, in case you didn't know, I really love that kid. Surprise!

Well, I guess I had better go for now. I need some ole shut-eye. Be sweet, and let me hear from you. I love you all very much.

The "you name it and I'll tell you what to feed it kid,"

Corky

I would even miss Father's Day in 1946, but I sent a belated note to Dad that said this:

Dear Dad,

This is a rather belated Father's Day greeting. I didn't forget you, but so many things have been happening that I haven't had time to

*write you. Boy, we have been busy all day long &
part of the night, too.*

*Dad, I just want to tell you how much I love
you. And I want to thank you for all you have
done for me. I haven't always appreciated it the
way I should, but I sure do tonight. You've
always been so good to me and, Pop, I haven't
forgotten all the lessons you taught me. But I
thank you most of all for the love you have given
to me and the other boys. God bless you, Dad.*

*Take care of Juanita and Mom for me. Know
that I love you.*

Corky

After arriving in Yokohama, I applied to the 11th Airborne
Division Jump School, which was in Sapporo on the northern
Japanese island of Hokkaido. I couldn't really tell you why I did
that, since I had no burning desire to be a paratrooper, and I
hadn't ever been up in an airplane before, but I supposed I
needed to find some kind of niche for myself. If nothing else,
there would be some prestige attached to being a part of the 11th
Airborne, which had first been activated in Europe in 1943, but
then was transferred to the Pacific Theater in 1944.

It saw action in Leyte in the Philippines, as well as in the
invasion of Luzon in January of 1945. Though labeled
"airborne," it acted in an infantry role on both occasions but later
participated in airborne operations. Its first paratroop drop was
on the Tagaytay Ridge in the Philippines, and from there the
division aided in the liberation of Manila, the Philippines capital
city. Two companies of its paratroopers raided the Los Banos
internment camp in February of 1945 and liberated over two
thousand civilians. Like I said, there was prestige attached to
being a part of that group.

It was important to me to be a part of something like that,

even though combat operations in the Pacific had ended even before the formal signing of the Japanese surrender on September 2, 1945. In addition to prestige, there was a sense of comradery, of brotherhood, to be a member of a group like that, with its short but storied history, much like being a Poly Parrot on one of the school's best teams in history.

At least that's how it felt to me as an 18-year-old abroad for the first time.

I was accepted into the 11th after passing the required physical and was transferred to the Adjutant General section at Division Headquarters in Sapporo on the northern Japanese island of Hokkaido. It was there that I had my first experience of flying in an airplane, although, remarkably, that stint required me to jump out of it. In fact, I ultimately had to jump out of five airplanes in order to earn my "jump pin" and qualify for the title "paratrooper."

The last four jumps seemed like old hat after the first one, though. That one, I'll never forget.

To get us used to the idea of committing ourselves to something so seemingly flimsy as nylon involved some education none of us had previously been exposed to. Although parachutes had originally been made of canvas, a sturdy fabric, a shift to silk reduced the weight of the canopies and made them more packable, even though the fabric was just as sturdy. Or so we were told. It sure didn't seem sturdy, though. Logistically, and maybe ironically, the problem was that the biggest source of silk for those canopies had been Japan. Of course, waging war against Japan severely restricted that market, so the U.S. Army had to come up with an acceptable substitute. Hence, another seemingly improbable shift, this time from silk to nylon.

Then came the task of educating us to a belief in committing ourselves to a fabric I had always thought was limited to being used in women's hosiery worn by the likes of pin-up girl Betty Grable. My recollection, too, was that they were susceptible to "running," partial tears caused by the slightest little snag, including a fingernail, that would then "run" up or down the leg from there, extending the tear. I had even been told it was why women shaved their legs, so as to avoid leg hair causing runs. Yeah, who wouldn't want to jump from an airplane with that material strapped to your back as the only thing between you and smashing to earth?

My group of future paratroopers was required to attend classroom study where we were taught how the chutes were assembled and how they worked. Then we sat, rapt, and watched as our instructors showed us how to pack the chutes into canvas backpacks. Next came hands-on instruction as we, ourselves, packed our assigned chutes into similar backpacks. This was all intended to give us confidence in them, at least intellectually, before we ever stepped out the door of a plane with the packs strapped to our backs.

When the assigned day for our first jump arrived, we gathered that pre-dawn morning in a hangar on the outskirts of Sapporo, where a large twin-engine Curtiss C-46 awaited. The C-46 started as a C-20, originally designed by the Curtiss-Wright Corporation for private use to compete with similar aircraft produced by Douglas and Boeing, but it had been adapted for military use after the outbreak of World War II. The C-46A was intended as a cargo plane, but by the latter years of the war, a new model, the C-46D, was in use, fitted with an extra door specifically designed to facilitate egress – that means jumping out of – by paratroopers.

Tables had been set up in the hangar, and rows of packed canvas bags, which held the nylon chutes that we had personally packed, lined the tops. We were usually a boisterous, talkative group, but the entire collection of us fell mute, struck dumb by the reality of what we were about to do. Even the most animated among us were silenced by the looming jump.

We grabbed our assigned chutes and began the somewhat

arduous task of donning them. They didn't slip on like a simple backpack would but had straps that went between our legs as well as straps across our torsos and backs. I struggled to strap mine on snugly and adjusted the harness to ensure I didn't slide out of the chute before the canopy could open. After all, that first step was a doozy, and I didn't want to make any miscalculations.

There were a few wisecracks as we geared up, then silence overtook us again. We had been divided into groups, or "sticks," of ten men each, and we followed our instructor's orders and entered the plane by stick, clambering up into the belly of the C-46. We quickly found our seats on benches lined along the walls of the plane and sat, silently, awaiting take-off.

I thought of Juanita and my family back in Fort Worth and thought what a great story this would be to tell when I returned home. Maybe even to ultimately tell my children and grandchildren. Assuming, of course, that I had packed my chute properly and put it on correctly and snugly and it opened like it was supposed to and I landed safely on the Japanese soil beneath me. Or, again assuming, of course, that the engine on the C-46 didn't fail and nosedive us into that same soil. I had been in automobile accidents before, even broken my nose – or rebroken, since I had first broken it playing football – in one, but the last thing I ever wanted to happen to me was to be a passenger in a plane crash. I believed that I could go a whole lifetime without experiencing that.

I looked around at my buddies and saw they were just as tense and scared as I was. All the ground-level bravado, and there were plenty of blowhards in the group, had long since faded. The engines roared and the C-46 lurched into motion. From where I sat, I could see out the open door, which didn't exactly bolster confidence. One lurch and twist of the plane and a group of unseatbelted paratrooper wannabees might get an early start on their way to the ground.

The plane gathered momentum, and I could see the concrete

runway whir by, melted from distinction into a soft blur. Then it dropped beneath us, out of sight, as we lifted off and became airborne. I leaned into my chute wedged between my back and the wall of the plane and tried to make myself as comfortable as possible. I learned quickly that there was no possibility of comfort. There were no cushioned seats, no stewardesses, no creature comforts of any kind. It was a stark reminder to me that this was not a pleasure trip and that I wouldn't be returning to the ground the same way I had left it.

As we neared the drop zone, or DZ, someone started an off-key rendition of the "Wabash Cannonball" in a raspy baritone voice. Legend had it that the song had been made up by anonymous hoboes who illegally hitched rides on trains across the United States in the late 19th Century, even though no one ever actually heard of a train called the Wabash Cannonball. According to the lyrics, the train supposedly "glides along the woodlands, through hills and by the shore . . . from the great Atlantic Ocean to the wild Pacific shore." Everyone knew the words, probably made most famous by The Carter Family in 1929, and more recently by Roy Acuff, so we all joined in. I could sing a little, as could a few of the others, but for the most part, it was a terrible choir. Still, it lifted our spirits and took our minds off the upcoming jump. Or maybe "drop" was a better word; we wouldn't really be doing any actual jumping, which implies going up.

Good thing whoever started the singing hadn't decided to go with "The Wreck of the Old '97," which left the engineer "dead in the wreck with his hand on the throttle, scalded to death by the steam." Better to be aboard the Wabash Cannonball than Old '97.

The sharp clang of a bell penetrated the drone of the engines and signaled an abrupt end to our singing. It meant that we were over the DZ.

"Stick one, stand and up and hook up," the jumpmaster

barked.

The first stick of ten men stood, stomping their boots on the floor of the plane. They let out a collective growl, calling on inner resources to bolster their courage. A cable, or static-line, ran parallel along the outer wall. Each man hooked a snap fastener to the cable, which would automatically pull the cord to release the chute when they jumped. It ensured no one would freeze and forget to release his own chute. What a horrible last mistake of your life that might be.

I watched closely, memorizing faces. One from Tucson, one from Schenectady, one from Oklahoma City. A couple from Texas – San Antonio and Wichita Falls. Two Californians, Los Angeles and San Bernardino. A Detroit native, a Louisianan from some small town near New Orleans, and an Ashville, North Carolinian. I wanted to see each of those faces again on the ground. Alive.

"Check equipment," the jumpmaster said.

Each man made a last minute check to ensure their chutes had been put away correctly, though it was too late at that point to unpack and repack, followed by a hand check to ensure all harnesses and straps were secure. With no obvious signs of problems, each man sounded off.

"Close it up and stand in the door."

The stick of men bunched closer to each other until the front man was standing directly in the open doorway, the second close behind, chest against the parachute of the man in front, and so forth.

A buzzer sounded. The jumpmaster said, "Go!" and slapped the front man on the thigh. That man then kicked out into the cold air, closely followed by his stick-mates, one right after the other like falling dominoes.

The plane banked and I craned my neck to look through the opening and see the short parade of men falling.

Chutes began to open. I counted: one . . . two . . . three . . .

four . . . five . . . six . . . seven . . . eight . . . nine . . . ten.

They all had opened.

I breathed a big sigh of relief. Seeing all ten chutes open upped my level of confidence in my own chute.

The bell sounded again as the C-46 completed its arc, then straightened out and re-entered the DZ.

"Stick two, stand up and hook up."

That was my stick. I was first up. I stomped my boots on the floor of the plane and tried to growl, but only an anguished *aarrgh* came out.

I stepped across the way to the door. All tension had fled. This was action time. I snapped my snap-fastener to the static-line and awaited orders.

"Check equipment."

I had already run a check on the ground and multiple times since we had taken off, but I did it again. Couldn't be too careful. Harness and straps felt snug.

"Close it up and stand in the door."

I centered myself in the doorway, hands on the sides of the opening. Behind me, I could feel the breath of the next man, just inches away. As I stood there in the doorway, looking down on the Hokkaido landscape, I remember asking myself, "Farris, what in the world are you doing so far away from Texas?"

The buzzer sounded. The jumpmaster said "Go" and slapped my thigh.

I stepped out into a cold blast of air that sucked the breath out of my lungs. Below me, I could still see open canopies of the preceding stick as those men neared the ground. I heard the shuffle of boots behind me and the metallic ring of snap-fasteners on cable as my stick mates followed me out the door.

A *whooshing* sound. Then a sickening lurch upward. I felt as if my torso had been yanked away from my legs, which swung limply beneath me.

I looked up. My chute was open.

Juanita had some beautiful dresses that I had seen her wear to church. So had other women from Poly Baptist. But I had never in my life seen a piece of fabric as beautiful as that opened nylon canopy that held me in its grip and slowly delivered me downward. Beautiful. Just beautiful.

And I told it so all the way to the ground.

Yeah, the ground. I hit it with a jolt, boots slamming hard. I buckled my knees and rolled sideways as we had been trained, then came to a stop. I took stock of myself and my surroundings. A little sore, but my legs moved as I struggled to my feet. Full feeling and sensation in all my limbs.

Safely on the ground. Just like I had been taught. Just like it had been drawn up in the playbook.

Not nose up against a tree, with dead legs.

"So," Gabe said, "jumping out of a perfectly good airplane sounded like a good idea to you?"

He leaned back against a tree, arms folded across his chest. He had a smug smile on his face, more of a smirk, really. He had a way of getting under my skin like very few people before him had been able to do. But I figured I could give as well as receive.

"Beats flying them into the ground," I said, returning his smirk. Man, even that hurt.

"Yeah, I guess you're right. I guess it's better to have at least a little control over how you touch down."

"That, it does."

"But riddle me this, preacher. At what point did you decide it was safe to jump out of that plane?"

"I don't understand your question. I didn't have a choice, so there was no decision to make."

"Well, here's what I'm getting at. Did you have confidence that your chute would work right and get you safely down?"

"I guess so."

"What gave you that confidence? By that, I mean, when did you start believing *in* your parachute instead of just believing *about* it?"

I had never thought of that before, and it got me to thinking. Did I even really believe *about* my parachute? Yeah, I guess I did. After all, I had been through classroom instruction about the process, and I had seen the experts pack and unpack and repack the chutes and explain how they worked. I had even packed my own chute, which gave me a sense of control over the process. I knew how it was supposed to work, and I was dead sure I had done it exactly like the instructor told us. That gave me a level of comfort that it would work when the time came. I supposed that meant I believed about it – what it was and how it worked.

Then, once we got over the drop zone, I watched as the first stick of ten men jumped, then I counted chutes. Ten paratroopers, ten open chutes. That reinforced my belief that the chutes would open. Of course, none of those had been my chute.

"I guess it wasn't until I stepped out of that plane and committed myself lock-stock-and-barrel to my chute, even though I had never seen that specific chute in action, that I moved from believing *about* it and started to believe *in* it."

"Sort of a metaphor for faith, isn't it?" Gabe asked.

"Where are you going with this?"

"I think you can figure that out for yourself, preacher," he said.

He vanished again.

Then it hit me what Gabe was getting at. And he was exactly right. Faith wasn't believing *about* something; it was about believing *in* something. In the New Testament, Hebrews called it "the evidence of things not seen."

I thought of another New Testament verse from the Book of James about believing in God. In the King James Version, it said, *"Thou believest that there is one God; thou doest well. The devils also believe, and tremble."* Or, as the New International

Version put it: "*You believe that there is one God. Good! Even the demons believe that – and shudder.*"

In other words, here I was on the floor of the Big Thicket with a broken back, with no assurance things were going to work out, and I had to decide whether I was still going to have faith. Faith *in* God, not merely faith that he existed. The latter wouldn't stand me apart from the devils. My circumstances may have been out of my control, but the decision about my faith was totally up to me.

CHAPTER THIRTEEN

As before, when Gabe pulled one of his vanishing acts, he really got me to thinking. This time, I went back in my mind to Corky Bo's birthday when he turned five, right in the middle of our tenure as missionaries to Japan. We were living in a compound in the Nishi-okubo district in the Shinjuku-ku ward of northern Tokyo, along with a number of other American, mostly missionary, families. It was an interesting time in our young family's life and it led to the missionary version of "keeping up with the Joneses."

It worked this way: A family in the compound would come up with some new gizmo or toy for their kids and, before you knew it, another family matched it for their kid. Then another and another, until every kid had one just like it. We all played the game. It was bad enough that our kids were living in a foreign country, far away from home and grandparents and aunts and uncles, so we parents wanted them to have material things to help them get along.

As long as it wasn't too expensive.

Corky Bo was one of four boys about the same age who formed a little clique there on the compound, wearing cowboy outfits or baseball uniforms, playing with each other, having sleepovers, and digging holes. I had never seen so many holes dug in my life, but all of them seemed to love putting a little shovel in the earth and turning dirt. We probably could have used some like them as part of the war effort, digging trenches and foxholes for the troops. The "Dirty Four" I dubbed them, because they usually ended up wearing as much dirt as they left behind.

Well, Corky Bo's fifth birthday was drawing near, and Juanita and I began discussing what to get him. We had always seemed to delight him in the past with something or other, like a bat and ball or a cowboy holster and six-shooters, even a stuffed monkey he named "Every Presley," his mangled pronunciation of "Elvis." We were sure we could turn the trick again.

Then I came home one day and there, at the home of one of his friends, I saw it: a bright, shiny new bicycle. I knew it was expensive, relatively speaking, and I wasn't sure how his parents were able to afford it—sent a prayer letter to their congregation back home, I supposed. That was the usual route for raising money, and surely they couldn't otherwise afford it on their missionary salary—which was the same as mine, and I sure couldn't afford it. We had bought him a Los Angeles Dodgers baseball uniform the year before, the Dodgers having just recently moved from Brooklyn a few years prior. It bore number 14, the number that belonged to Gil Hodges and, when Corky Bo wore it, he always referred to himself as "Ol' Gil."

But a bicycle wasn't a baseball uniform. This was in a totally different category.

"I'm putting my foot down," I told Juanita. "We don't have to buy something just because someone else did."

"I know, honey," she said, but her tone suggested she didn't believe either one of us. If one of the Dirty Four had a new bicycle, it was just a matter of time before the other three would, including our son.

A few days later, another new bicycle showed up on the compound. Two down out of the four. And then a third. By now, every one of the Dirty Four had a new bicycle except my son. And that really irked me. I loved my boy as much as any of those other fathers. So, Juanita and I sat down and figured out how we could swing a bicycle. We finally decided if we cut back on some things for ourselves, went ahead and sent a prayer letter back home, maybe even missed a meal or two, we could scrape up enough to buy a bicycle just like all his friends. I was kidding about missing meals, but money was really tight for us in Japan.

Once Juanita and I decided to make the purchase, I was determined to milk it for all I could. So, I called Ol' Gil into the den one day—he was wearing his ever-present Dodgers jersey, which was in bad need of a washing—sat him down on the couch and said, "You know your birthday's coming up."

"Yes, sir."

Of course he did. What a stupid question! What kid didn't know when his birthday was? But I pressed ahead.

"If you could have anything you wanted, what would you like for your birthday?"

He thought for a minute, his little forehead furrowed. Then he said, "I'd like a chicken feather."

I thought my hearing had failed me. "A what?"

"A chicken feather."

"A chicken feather?"

"Yes, sir. A chicken feather."

"What on earth would you want a chicken feather for?"

"Well, sometimes we play cowboys and Indians, and I like to be an Indian. This way I can wear the chicken feather on my head like an Indian."

How do you deal with that? I said, "Now, son, I'm serious. What do you really want for your birthday?"

"I want a chicken feather."

I felt my temper starting to rise a little, which wasn't good. He was just a little boy, and I knew he couldn't really understand what was going on. I decided to toss him a clue.

"I mean if you could have anything—I mean *anything*—even a brand new bicycle, what would you want? I'm serious."

"I'm serious, too. I want a chicken feather."

Gabe reappeared about an hour later. He seemed to come and go as he pleased.

"Miss me?" he asked.

"Gave me time to think without your incessant chatter."

"Okay. Well, then, penny for your thoughts."

"I think you're right about the parachute-faith metaphor. And I've come up with another one. As long as I'm lying here trying to figure out why this happened."

He listened patiently while I then told him the story of Corky Bo and the chicken feather.

"Interesting kid," he said when I was finished.

"You have no idea."

"So, what's your metaphor?"

"Three guesses what he got for his birthday that year."

"I'm guessing it wasn't the chicken feather. Bicycle?"

"Got it on the first guess. We gave him the bicycle whether he wanted it or not."

"I bet he wasn't too disappointed."

"He liked the bicycle, all right, but he sure wanted that chicken feather. I think maybe he really was disappointed that he didn't get it. Maybe that's what we should have gotten him. Then he could have learned a lesson about misplaced expectations."

"Yeah, that would have been great. Use your five-year-old kid for philosophical lessons just to make a point."

I laughed. "Yeah, I suppose that might not have been the best thing."

Gabe shook his head. "No, you did the right thing. Soon enough that feather would have rotted away or he would have lost it and then have nothing to show for it. He would have wished he had that bicycle. He might not have fully appreciated it then, but you knew what was best for him. That's what dads do, even if it doesn't seem like it to the kid at the time."

I nodded. "I know that. But lying out here in the middle of the woods, flat on my back, has gotten me to thinking about that story again. And it's made me wonder about a different metaphor than the one about parachutes."

"Okay, now we're getting there. Lay it on me."

"Am I here because God wanted to give me a bicycle and I asked for a chicken feather instead?"

"I'm not sure I follow you."

"Isn't that what happened to Jonah? God wanted him to go to Nineveh, but Jonah decided to go to Tarshish instead. And he ended up in the belly of a whale. Maybe God wanted me to do something else with my life, maybe go back to Japan, and instead, I decided to come to Texas just because I wanted to come home. Maybe I tried to convince myself I was following God's will, but what if I was really just following my own wants? What if Japan was my bicycle and Texas was my chicken feather? Maybe my belly of a whale happens to be the Big Thicket."

Gabe started shaking his head before I had even finished. "So you think God is punishing you for something? Punishing you for preaching the gospel in Texas instead of preaching it in Japan? That doesn't make sense. Sometimes bad things happen, and they have nothing to do with punishment. Isn't that just life?"

"I agree that not every time something bad happens, it directly correlates to disobeying God. But I also have to consider the possibility that, in this case, it does."

"I suppose if you can figure that out, then you can pray your way back, can't you? Apologize for taking a wrong turn and promise to do what you should have done in the first place? Assuming you did something wrong, which I don't buy. But isn't that what Jonah did in the belly of the whale? Prayed himself out?"

"I don't know if I can figure it out."

"Well, doesn't it defeat the purpose of punishment if you can't see a connection? That makes it seem arbitrary. And God's not arbitrary, is he?"

"No, I don't believe He is."

"So, why would He hide the ball? Let's take this logically. Let's start by tracing your steps and all the decisions you've made that led you here."

"Where do we start?"

"Let's start with you and Juanita getting married. Isn't that also about the time you entered the ministry?"

"Yeah."

"So, what was the first big decision you made?"

"I suppose that was the decision to preach instead of going into the music ministry."

"I guess that explains why you sometimes sing as part of your sermons."

"Yeah. I still feel that music is an important part of my ministry."

"Hard to see how God would be unhappy about that."

"That's sure what I thought."

"And you still haven't explained to me how all this led you back to Japan as a missionary. Walk me through the decision-making process."

CHAPTER FOURTEEN

It really wasn't until I spent some time in Sapporo on the island of Hokkaido, where I had been assigned to the Adjutant General's section at Division Headquarters, that I really came to know Japan. Sapporo was far more primitive than Tokyo or Yokohama, and it seemed as if I had been transported back in time fifty or a hundred years. I supposed war would do that. American bombing sorties had damaged considerable portions of ports along the island's southern coastline, which separated Hokkaido from the largest, and main, Japanese island of Kyushu. Had the war not ended when it did, Russian forces were preparing to invade Hokkaido. That would have been devastating.

Sapporo was the capital city of Hokkaido Prefecture. Prefectures were official subdivisions in Japan, much like we have states, with their own elected governors and legislative bodies. Located in the southwestern portion of the island, in the alluvial fan of the Toyohira River, the city of about 700,000 people was situated just across the portion of the Sea of Japan that separated Hokkaido from the Asian mainland. In fact, it was less than 500 miles from Sapporo to Vladivostok in the Soviet Union, about the distance from Amarillo, Texas, to Austin.

As I adjusted to my work in Sapporo and became more efficient at my job duties, I found that I had more free time. I spent most of it walking up and down the streets, visiting some little shops near the base and getting to know the Japanese people. I found them to be friendly and curious, and I experienced very little animosity from them despite my presence in their city as part of an occupying military force. I wasn't sure I could have done the same had I been in their place, although I gathered from many of them that they were just grateful the war had ended. In fact, most of them had never wanted to be in a war with the United States in the first place.

As winter approached, I even had a few occasions to venture into the countryside on skiing trips. That wasn't something you got much of a chance to do in Texas. Years later, during our missionary service on Hokkaido, I thought about those skiing trips when I took my two older kids out and taught them to ski. We had a very likeable chaplain stationed with us on the base in Sapporo, though he wasn't much of a preacher. Certainly not like a young man I had heard preach at Poly Baptist the prior New Year's Eve. Still, I attended his chapel services regularly, along with a few of the other men. I found myself subjected to some good-natured teasing from a lot of men about going to chapel, but when I fell in with these others who were of like mind when it came to our faith, I developed some good friendships.

Unfortunately, attending worship services was primarily about comradery for me, getting a chance to meet and mix with like-minded others, rather than any deeply rooted sense of responsibility to meet the spiritual needs of the Japanese people. My interaction with them was friendly but not personal and certainly not on a spiritual level. It was hard to explain why that was so, especially given that New Year's Eve sermon I had heard less than a year prior by a young preacher who had inspired me. The closest I came was when Christmas of 1945 rolled around.

I never felt more alone than that year, stuck there in frigid Hokkaido over 6,000 miles away from Fort Worth and Juanita. I went with the chaplain and some of my buddies to a small Japanese church for a pageant just two days before Christmas. The tiny building that served as the church was nothing more than a ramshackle affair, little more than a lean-to. Unpainted, ancient, and miserably cold, freezing winds easily and freely penetrated large gaps between the boards that poorly served as walls.

The first time I walked inside, pulling my coat tightly around me to stay warm, I thought of the fine churches I had been in back in Fort Worth, including Sagamore Hill Baptist and Poly Baptist, with brick and mortar walls, well-insulated, and outfitted with heat and air conditioning, cushioned pews, and overhead lighting. For maybe the first time, I felt a touch of pity for these Japanese Christians, making do as best they could in a country devastated by the effects of war. Pity, and maybe a touch of guilt, too.

The church members welcomed us warmly, even though we were literally their conquerors, and they did their best to make us feel at home. They made a point to give us the seats closest to a wood-burning stove, themselves taking seats farther away from the stove's meager warmth.

The pageant, itself, was presented by the children, playing the roles of Mary, Joseph, the Wise Men, and Shepherds, and heralding the birth of Jesus in a manger that may well have provided, for all its poverty, more comfort than these children were experiencing in post-war Japan. They were so cute, and at the same time pathetic, and I found my heart touched by their need. I daresay, I even began to feel the embers of love for them, embers that simply needed a little oxygen to burst into flames.

I thought of my comfortable life back in Texas. Though the Farrises weren't a wealthy family, by any means, I had never wanted for anything I needed. That didn't mean I got everything I wanted, but even as a boy I had been able to distinguish between want and need.

I wondered what life could possibly offer these children in war-devastated Japan. And, again for the first time, I wondered if maybe I had something to offer them.

"So this Christmas pageant with these Japanese kids playing Mary and Joseph. Were these Christian kids?" Gabe asked.

"I don't know. They were so young, just little kids, but they were part of this Christian mission there. I guess their folks might have been."

"Salvation through family lineage, eh?"

"No, of course not. But they stood a better chance of someday becoming Christians than kids who didn't have Christian parents. No guarantees, but certainly better possibilities."

Gabe thought about that for a moment. "The reason why I asked is because I always thought most of Japan was Buddhist or Shinto. Especially back then."

"It was then and it still is now."

"That's got me wondering if those kids even knew what they were doing in that pageant. What did they know about shepherds and wise men and babies in mangers?"

"Would it matter if they didn't know anything?"

"You tell me, preacher. Is it sacrilegious for non-Christians to co-opt a Christian holiday? I hear people complaining all the time about using Xmas instead of Christmas and taking Christ out of Christmas. You got any thoughts on that?"

I thought back to some of the things I had learned in my classes at the seminary, as well as in my Greek classes at Baylor. I couldn't blame Gabe for getting his facts wrong. It was a common misconception among a lot of Christians.

"Here's the thing about that," I said. "The X doesn't take Christ out of Christmas. It stands for the Greek letter *chi*, which is the first letter in 'Christ.' It's actually symbolic of Christ and the cross, and it has nothing to do with taking Christ out of Christmas. I've even read that a lot of Jewish immigrants coming in to the United States at Ellis Island were illiterate, but they refused to sign their names with an X. They thought that was sacrilegious because of what the X stood for. Instead they used an O, what they called in Yiddish a *kikel* for circle."

"Well, aren't you the educated one!"

"A lot of it might be useless information, but if I didn't have it packed into my brain, we couldn't have this conversation."

"And here I thought using the X was because people were either too lazy to spell out the whole word or they just wanted to celebrate the holiday without buying in to the theology behind it."

"There's some truth to that idea about not wanting to spell out the whole word, but not like you'd think. After the printing press was first invented by Gutenberg, they had to set type for the press by hand. To save time, and money, the church starting using the X as an abbreviation for Christ. So, in some religious literature, you might even sometimes see Xian and Xianity instead of Christian and Christianity."

"Who'd a thunk I'd be dead in a forest learning all this stuff! Obviously, my public school education was lacking." He seemed to think about that for a minute, then said, "But surely, you're not telling me most people today know all this background. I bet the ones that write X-M-A-S aren't doing it to honor Christ, but they're doing it either as a shortcut or a way to deliberately cut Christ out of the equation. After all, Christmas is so commercialized, sometimes it's hard to know it has any religious significance at all. It's all about buying and selling stuff. Doesn't that sorta frost you a little bit?"

"Sure it does. But you know what frosts me—to use your term—even more?"

"Pray tell."

"It's Christians getting their noses all bent out of joint because someone who's not a Christian celebrates Christmas or some other holiday around the same time. My job is to spread the gospel, but not to ram it down everybody's throat. If someone else wants to celebrate a different holiday, or not celebrate at all, or celebrate Christmas for their own reasons, it's no skin off my nose. It doesn't change my beliefs or how I choose to serve the Lord. I suspect I present a far better witness of my faith by simply living it than I do by raging at anyone who doesn't believe the same way I do and trying to make them feel bad because they don't."

"Makes sense to me. I wish it did to a lot more Christians."

"That's why it wouldn't have bothered me if those Japanese kids in the pageant had no idea what they were doing. It may well have been the first time they were ever exposed to the Christmas story, and it's better that they were than if they weren't. It was a seed, and who knew when it would grow? Sometimes we harvest, but sometimes we simply plant and someone else harvests later. But there's no harvest without the planting."

Gabe thought on that for a spell. He got off the stump he had been sitting on and walked in a slow circle around the spot where I lay. I swiveled my head to follow him.

When he had completed a revolution around me, he sat back on the stump.

"Okay," he said, "I think I got you a little off topic. Let's get back to checking out all your decisions."

"It's not really off topic. Japan's got a lot to do with how I got here today. And to give you a sneak preview of my thinking, I'm starting to wonder if I'm here because I was supposed to be in Japan right now, not Texas. Like I said before, maybe Texas was my chicken feather and this is my belly of a whale."

"Let's work through it logically." He smiled and added, "I know you're all about faith, and faith isn't necessarily logical, but let's do the analysis my way, anyway."

Following the Christmas pageant at that pitiful little church in Sapporo, several of my buddies and I decided to buy some toys and play Santa Claus for the children who had entertained us, but something prevented my participation in those plans. The day before Christmas, I was notified by Headquarters in Tokyo that I had been granted an emergency furlough and would be provided air transportation back to the States. The communique merely stated that the furlough had been granted because of "serious illness at home," but it failed to specify who was sick or what the nature of the illness was.

After hurriedly packing and leaving Sapporo for Tokyo, I spent a lonely Christmas day at the replacement depot before finally boarding a plane for the flight home two days later. I was still totally in the dark. I hadn't been able to call home, so I had no idea which family member was ill, what the illness was, or how serious it was. The uncertainty was killing me. I thought it was most likely one of my parents who, though not elderly by most standards, were nevertheless approaching their sixties. Surely not my brothers. They were too young. Buddy was in his late 20s and Webber in his early 30s, though I certainly understood that illness had no respect for age. Just witness my own health issues as a boy. But they were both in perfect health, as far as I knew. No, either Mom or Dad made the most sense.

The real question involved that ambiguous word "serious." As I sat in the fuselage of a massive four-engine Douglas C-54 Skymaster transport plane, awaiting take-off from Haneda Air Base near Tokyo, my imagination unleashed. Worst case scenarios flitted through my mind, but at least I was going home to Texas. I couldn't get there soon enough.

As I awaited take-off, through a window I watched a diminutive Japanese man wearing a *kasa*, a straw coolie hat, as he labored in a field at the end of the runway. I wasn't sure exactly what he was doing, but it was obvious that it was back-breaking physical labor as he wielded a hoe or some other sort of chopping tool.

I had a "there but for the grace of God" moment as I watched. I realized how fortunate I was to live in a country like the United States that provided me with opportunities that laborer couldn't even imagine. Opportunities that I had, up until then, taken for granted. I had been given a scholarship that would provide me with a first-rate education at a first-rate university. A chance to play football, a game I loved, one that had earned me adulation in high school. I was sure that poor Japanese worker would have traded almost anything to have been given that same opportunity to go to school and to play games instead of chopping weeds in a field by a runway. I not only had taken my opportunity for granted, but I had also thrown it away by dropping out of school.

The engines roared and the C-54 began to move. Slowly at first then it picked up speed and barreled down the runway. I kept my eyes on the Japanese worker as we approached him, then I watched him disappear as we lifted upward. With a sense of relief, I turned away from the window. I figured that would be the last Japanese I would ever see. I couldn't have been happier.

But that would change.

I later wrote in a college paper at Baylor University: "I was tired of the whole country. I was tired of the people, the poverty, the hunger, the destruction, the everlasting stench, the narrow streets, the unpainted houses, the indescribable filth, the hopelessness that hems in the lightest heart. I had seen enough of Japan . . . I hated it. I never wanted to see those islands again. This was good-bye for keeps—or so I thought."

CHAPTER FIFTEEN

From my vantage point on the floor of the Big Thicket, I could tell from what little of the sun was visible overhead that it was sinking into the western sky. That meant night was coming, with a corresponding drop in temperatures. It occurred to me that I should seek some sort of shelter for the coming hours. I still had Gabe's cigarette lighter, but nothing to burn except leaves. That seemed too dangerous. At least the night before, I had been able to confine my fire to the interior of my briefcase in a small clearing, but something out in the open posed too great a threat of cinders spreading. Unless I could dig a hole deep enough to serve as a fire pit. I had already dug one hole, seeking water, but the effort had been exhausting. I wasn't sure I had it in me to duplicate the feat.

I spotted an area of undergrowth encircling a few trees that looked promising. If I could snuggle my way inside, it might serve as a cave of sorts, albeit a leaky, drafty cave. Still, it might provide some protection from the wind. And I might be able to pull enough leaves on top of me to serve as a rudimentary blanket.

I angled my body in that direction and got on the move again.

"I'll bet you're wishing you were back in Japan about now."

I heard Gabe's voice before I saw his boots as they circled the undergrowth I was aiming for and walked toward me. He looked back over his shoulder.

"That where you're going?" he asked.

I nodded and kept moving. When you moved as slowly as I did, you didn't have time to stop and chat; you chatted on the go. He stood and watched as I neared the undergrowth. He looked skyward, then back at me as I reached the edge of the growth and rolled onto my back to rest.

"I reckon it's gonna get cold again," he said.

"Your powers of observation amaze me," I said. "It is January, after all."

He sat on the ground facing me and leaned against a tree. "I've been thinking about your story," he said, "and here's what I don't get. When you left Japan, you told yourself it was for good, but that turned out not to be the case. So, why did you go back?"

"It's a little hard to explain. I'm not sure I fully understand it, myself."

"Give it a try."

I had a chance to do a lot of thinking during that long flight across the Pacific. I still didn't know who in my family was ill, but I had to face the possibility that one of my loved ones might well be at death's door and could even have already entered by the time I got there. After all, the army didn't hand out emergency furloughs like candy. An emergency furlough usually meant that . . . well, that there was an emergency. As I sat on that plane, worrying, I came face-to-face with the reality that death was inevitable in every family. Even mine. Sure, I had lost friends before, but not a close family member.

That got me thinking about a very familiar passage of scripture, one I knew by heart even as a rebellious teenager. Psalms 23. I had memorized it during vacation Bible school as a child and could still recite it on the spot if called to. I had never really thought about its meaning before. It was more like a poem you had to learn in English class in school. You could recite the words by rote while remaining oblivious to the meaning. But now that familiar chapter took on new significance to me. Especially the part that said, "Yea, though I walk through the valley of the shadow of death . . ." The scripture didn't say, "Yea, *if* I walk through the valley of the shadow of death . . ." That might have been more comforting because it would have given death some uncertainty. But such was not the case.

Years later, I learned from my Hebrew and Old Testament classes in the seminary that the phrase could legitimately have been interpreted, "Yea, *when* I walk through the valley of the shadow of death . . . " Interpreted that way, there was a definite certainty to it. A blanket assertion that we, every last one of us, would all someday walk through that valley, either ourselves or with loved ones. The promise of the Twenty-third Psalm wasn't that we would bypass it, but rather that there would be comfort in the valley. "I will fear no evil, because Thou art with me." The promise was that, in the darkest shadows of that valley, there was a hand we could grab on to for support and guidance. And in the center of the palm of that hand, there was a scar.

Even though I hadn't yet gone off to seminary and submerged myself in what might seem to some as the mundane untangling of verb forms and conditional phrases, I latched on to that verse for comfort while sitting aboard that airplane. I feared that I might soon walk through the valley, but I also knew that whatever might be awaiting, it was out of my hands and in the Lord's.

That didn't stop me from rushing to the first telephone I saw, though, when I arrived in San Francisco to make a collect call home. I was greatly relieved to learn that, while my father had indeed suffered a serious heart attack, he was recuperating nicely in the hospital. By the time I reached Fort Worth, I found him well on the road to recovery. Though he did die a few years later at a still very young age in his early 60s, I was able to spend more time with him once I arrived home.

By this point, I had only one month left in my commitment to the army, and my furlough would occupy all but one week of that. So, I went ahead and enrolled at Texas Wesleyan College in Fort Worth, declaring a major in music, to prepare for a life of ministry in Christian music. I then started classes in January for the Spring 1947 semester. After taking a couple of days off for a quick trip to California in February for my final separation from the army, I returned and undertook my studies with far more seriousness than I had at SMU during my shortened football career.

It took a while for me to readjust to civilian life. Or maybe it was to adjust in the first place. At least as an adult, or at least as adult as one can feel at the age of nineteen, with my twentieth birthday looming in just a few months. One of the things that bothered me was a gnawing urge that, music major or not, what I really wanted to do was to preach. At first, I was certain that it was simply a personal desire. After all, I had never preached before. I wondered if maybe I had just been so taken with that New Year's Eve preacher I mentioned earlier, and whom I'll talk about later, that I was subconsciously wanting to emulate him. So I ignored the urge. I sure didn't know all there was to know about the ministry, but I knew enough to know that you didn't become a preacher just because you wanted to. You became a preacher because God had directed you to. It wasn't simply a career choice; it was a calling.

Besides, like I said, I had enrolled in college as a music major and surely I wasn't about to let that go to waste. Along with Dallas Alford and the other members of the Poly Baptist quartet— who, by the way, had welcomed me back with open arms; I wasn't sure if they really missed me or simply needed to plug that hole at tenor—I had made some very definite plans around full-time Christian music work. But believe it or not, it was through the quartet that I began to sense that my desire to preach was not simply my own initiative, but rather it was a desire that had been planted in my heart by the Lord.

In the spring of 1947, the quartet sang at the Texas Baptist Student Union state convention. While we were there, I had an opportunity to hear a moving sermon on Acts 9:6: *And he trembling and astonished said, Lord, what wilt thou have me to do? And the Lord said unto him, Arise, and go into the city, and it shall be told thee what thou must do.*

Then the preacher – another one who, like that New Year's Eve preacher, greatly influenced my life – said, "Everyone in this group tonight should ask God this question: 'Lord, what wilt thou have me to do?'"

I remember saying to myself, with smug self-assurance, "Yes, sir! He's right. Everyone here should ask the Lord that question."

Then it hit me that I had never really asked the Lord that, myself. I had surrendered to full-time service, so I thought I had done my duty, but I had never asked God exactly what He wanted me to do as part of that service. I just assumed that He wanted me in religious music because . . . well, because I could sing and that was what I liked doing. But now I had to ask myself whether that was really all there was to it, and whether I simply wanted that to be God's will for me because of personal preference.

Sure, I knew that God wanted me to use my talents for him—another Bible verse jumped out at me from vacation Bible school: *"As every man has received the gift, even so minister the same to one another."* I Peter 4:10—but that didn't mean I was limited to that. And maybe, just maybe, I had other talents, as well. Ones I didn't even know about yet.

When I got back home after the convention, I found myself a little bit shaken. I had been presuming that God's will for my life was based upon my own myopic self-assessment, and I hadn't really opened myself to the possibility that it might be something else, entirely. Maybe, I thought, that was where that strange urge to preach, something I had never done before, was coming from. So I began to pray, with an earnestness that I had never prayed with before. Not just pat expressions and token lip service to prayer, but genuinely, urgently seeking the Lord's will for my life.

I even found that I could no longer pay close attention to sermons at church on Sundays. Instead, every time the preacher got up to speak, I saw myself up there, behind the pulpit with an open Bible, imagining what I would say if I were the preacher. My desire to preach soon turned to a yearning. I wasn't sure I had ever "yearned" before, other than to be reunited with Juanita while I was overseas, but that was the kind of longing to preach I started to feel.

By the time summer rolled around, I was certain of my path. When I shared it with Juanita, she shocked me by saying, "I've known that for a while. I was just waiting for you to get there on your own without any pressure from me."

I didn't think about it this way at the time, but it turned out to be a monumental decision in terms of our future. We both knew this would mean changes in our immediate plans, but we really had no idea how far those changes would ultimately stretch. Nothing against Texas Wesleyan, a Methodist school, and its music program, but if I wanted to be a Baptist preacher, I needed the kind of Baptist education that would support it. That meant seminary on down the line but first it meant transferring to Baylor University in Waco, *the* Baptist college for turning out what I later learned were called "preacher boys."

We were to be married in June of 1947, and I wanted to transfer as soon as I could to Baylor, hopefully for the fall semester. But since Juanita already had a good job in Fort Worth, and she would be the primary source of our income while I was in school, we decided that I should go to Texas Wesleyan for one more year so we could stockpile a little money, then I would transfer to Baylor the following year.

We were married on June 27 at Poly Baptist Church, in a ceremony presided over by pastor Floyd B. Chaffin. My best man was one of my high school friends, and the groomsmen included both of my brothers, Webber and Buddy. Juanita's maid of honor was her friend Pollye West, and one of her bridesmaids was her little sister Janis, the youngest of the Peacock clan. According to the Fort Worth *Star-Telegram*:

The bride wore a white slipper satin gown with lace bodice and fingertip veil which fell from a heart-shaped halo of illusion and orange blossoms. She carried an orchid on a white Bible.

I sure didn't know much about wedding gowns, but I did know that she was the most beautiful bride in the history of Fort Worth. As of mid-January of 1965, in the Big Thicket, I was sure that truth still held.

After our wedding, we went to New Mexico for a brief honeymoon then returned to Fort Worth where I resumed classes at Texas Wesleyan College. In addition to my basics and music classes there, I also enrolled in a class in homiletics, defined as "the art of preaching"—who knew there was an art to it?—at Southwestern Baptist Theological Seminary in Fort Worth. We splurged and bought a car so I could drive between the two campuses for my daily classes. I even found a job at a downtown parking lot to help out with expenses. Even years later, I always had a hard time thinking of myself as "Corky the parking lot attendant."

While at Texas Wesleyan, and still with very little experience, and even less enthusiasm, primarily because of fear, I accepted a job as youth director at North Fort Worth Baptist Church. That allowed me to earn a little more money for the two of us, and also to exercise my strong suit in music. The position included handling the church's music program, since they were without a music director at the time, and that was the only part of the job I felt remotely qualified for. The hours were long and the work was hard, but I enjoyed every minute of it. It turned out to be a great place to gain experience from on-the-job training. I even led a citywide youth revival in Fort Worth and set up and conducted mission Bible schools around the city, using all volunteer help.

One of those Bible schools was located in a slum section of Fort Worth, and we used a convenient nearby bridge for the roof of an auditorium by meeting underneath it. A lot of the children who attended lived in the neighborhood in shacks and lean-tos. Poverty-stricken, they came to Bible school in dirty, ragged clothes. They were a rowdy lot but, bless their hearts, they were so hungry for someone to love them that they just swarmed all over us every morning when we arrived, for no other reason than because we had taken an interest in them.

It was those Bible schools, and spending time with those kids, that triggered a memory from Japan. For just a fleeting moment, caught in the flicker of my imagination. I looked at those kids in the Bible school and I almost found myself once again seated on a train coach somewhere between Sendai and Sapporo in northern Japan, looking through a window into the faces of other little children with ragged clothes. As we lumbered by, they gazed at the strange American soldiers who were enjoying the warmth of a train coach while they shivered in sub-freezing weather. That vivid memory set me to thinking: What about those little children in Japan, and the other ones who had so graciously put on the Christmas pageant for us?

It seemed as if, for the first time, I found myself truly concerned about the needs of Japan and the people I had seen and met over there, even though I had now been relocated thousands of miles away. Odd how the convenience of being near them hadn't triggered the concern, but it had taken returning to the States for that to happen. I asked myself: *Why doesn't someone go over there to tell them about Jesus?*

And then came the inevitable follow-up question, which reflected the danger of asking questions like that: *Why don't I?*

They were almost off-hand questions when I first asked them of myself, but they began to gnaw at me after I transferred from Texas Wesleyan to Baylor, where Juanita also enrolled and took classes. It seemed as if we, too, were living in poverty. We lived in a tiny apartment where you almost had to be careful when you put the key in the door to unlock it lest you break a window on the other side. But we both knew that our poverty was transitory, and not much different from many of our college friends. The day would come when we would graduate and move to a nicer house in a better part of some town. We always knew we would never get rich, at least not monetarily, but of course, that was never the goal. But those children in Japan were different. What future did they have? Even in that tiny apartment, I felt as if we lived as royalty compared to them.

While at Baylor, in addition to my classes and serving as pastor at the Ninth Street Mission, I made three summer mission trips to Japan with other college students from Texas before I obtained my B.A. in Greek in 1951. Juanita accompanied me on the last trip, the summer before graduation, and she told me that she almost immediately fell in love with the Japanese people as soon as she stepped off the plane. Just as I already had, although it took me a little longer. Several years longer.

Then, after graduating from Baylor, it was on to New Orleans Baptist Theological Seminary for the final phase of classroom training to be a preacher. But all the while, in the back of my mind, I kept thinking about Japan and the needs of the people there. Needs that I began to believe the Lord was leading me to try to help meet.

As the Old Testament prophet wrote in Isaiah 6:8: *Also I heard the voice of the Lord, saying, Whom shall I send, and who will go for us? Then said I, Here am I, send me.*

"What did you study at New Orleans?" Gabe asked.

"I specialized in Old Testament studies. I got my Bachelor of Divinity in 1955 then got my Doctor of Theology in 1958."

"Some folks would say the New Testament is a superior set of books."

"They're complementary to each other. But I'll admit there were some obscurities in the Old Testament I learned about." I laughed. "You should try to read my doctoral dissertation sometime."

"That bad, huh?"

I laughed again. "Yeah. The title of it was 'Degrees of Definiteness in the Aramaic Genitive Relationships in the Book of Daniel.'"

Gabe joined my laughter. "I think I'll wait for the movie."

"It'll be a long wait."

Gabe gestured around at the trees. "I can wait. I've got nothing better to do."

We stayed quiet for a while after that. I was surprised that he remained seated in front of the tree instead of disappearing like he was prone to do, but I welcomed even the silent company of a ghost/hallucination/angel. It helped ease the loneliness and took my mind off my family back in Duncanville.

After a few minutes of silence, he said, "How long after seminary was it before you went back to Japan again?"

"Not long. I had served as pastor of Goodwood Baptist Church in Baton Rouge—the founding pastor, in fact—while I was at New Orleans, and that's where both Darlyne and Corky Bo were born. In 1957, Juanita and I were both appointed by the Foreign Mission Board of the Southern Baptist Convention as full-time foreign missionaries. In the Spring of 1958, once I finalized my Th.D., our little family sailed aboard the ship *President Wilson* to Tokyo. From there, ultimately, the story leads . . . to here."

We lapsed into silence again as the sun continued to set. Soon the sky was dark.

Darker than Asashio's eyebrows.

CHAPTER SIXTEEN

When Darlyne and Corky Bo got home from school Wednesday afternoon, Juanita didn't tell them anything, nor had she said anything earlier to Stevie, because there really was nothing concrete to tell. She feared that Stevie might have picked up on her mood, her worry, but he seemed to be fine, playing with his cars. The last thing she wanted to do was to scare her kids into thinking something bad had happened to their daddy, so she encouraged them to keep busy in their rooms, since it was too cold to play outside. She asked Corky Bo to take Stevie with him into the room they shared, in order to get him out of the den, which opened to the kitchen. She didn't want them playing or watching television there because, if the phone rang with bad news, she wanted to be able to talk openly without them hearing.

And she certainly didn't want them to see her cry.

She fretted as she prepared supper that evening. One of their favorites was her beef stroganoff and rice recipe, so she set about making that. But now when one of the kids came in to ask "when's supper going to be ready," it would inevitably be followed by "when's Daddy going to get home?" She could answer the first question, but not the latter.

As she stood by the stove and stirred the stroganoff, she fought to hold back her emotions. It had now been hours since she had last talked to Byron Richardson and he told her that Corky and Gabe had taken off last night around ten. She looked at the clock on the stove, its hands reflecting that it was 5:31 in the afternoon. Getting dark outside. Nearly twenty hours since take-off and no word. She knew that meant only one of two things: they were somewhere where they simply couldn't access a telephone, or they were physically unable to call. The latter raised additional questions. Dark questions. Ones she really didn't want to hear answers to.

"When's supper going to be ready?"

It was Corky Bo. She hadn't heard him approach. She looked at him standing between the kitchen and the den, already wearing his flannel pajamas. Bedtime wasn't until 9:00, but he liked to wear them around the house because they were warm and comfortable.

"In about five minutes," she said. "Go tell Darlyne and Stevie, and y'all wash your hands and come on."

A few minutes later, supper was on the table. The kids took their assigned places, Corky Bo and Stevie on the side with their backs to the outer wall, with Darlyne across from them. Juanita sat at her place at the end of the table, facing an empty chair at the opposite end.

She held out her hands. Darlyne took one, Corky Bo the other. Stevie held Corky Bo's free hand and reached across the table to take Darlyne's. They bowed their heads.

"Lord, we thank you for this food we are about to receive and we ask your blessings on it and on us. We pray for your traveling mercy for Daddy as he returns home."

She fought back a sob. Was she being presumptuous in asking for that? Was it already too late?

"In Jesus name we pray. Amen."

They began to eat. Silently at first. She could see that the kids sensed something was wrong, but they didn't know what. They just knew something was off with their mommy.

"When's Daddy going to be home?" Darlyne asked.

And there it was. The unanswerable question Juanita had been deflecting all afternoon and evening.

"Soon," she said. She paused, then an urge to lay some groundwork for the bad news she was dreading took hold. "He should be here already. I don't know where they are."

Corky Bo looked at her and piped up in an unnaturally chipper voice. "Maybe they crashed."

"No!" she snapped. As soon as she did, she cringed. Corky

Bo shrank back, almost as if she had slapped him. "Don't say that," she said in a much softer tone. "They're just running late. That's all. I don't want you to think like that."

They ate the rest of their supper in total silence. Juanita knew in her heart of hearts that her son had nailed it. He didn't know it, but he had simply said what she had been thinking. She knew that they had crashed. There was no other possible explanation.

A tear coursed down her cheek.

CHAPTER SEVENTEEN

"Tyler County Sheriff's Office," the dispatcher said as she answered the phone in the small office in Woodville, county seat for Tyler County in southeast Texas. Although the office was small, it was a perfect fit for the location. After all, Tyler County was a small county, both in terms of area, scarcely 936 square miles—with the bulk of that comprised of timberlands—and population, numbering less than 13,000. It didn't take a large force to patrol the county or a large office to serve as home base.

"This is Hardin County Deputy Boyd over here in Kountze," the caller said. "We got a call from the pastor of one of the Baptist churches here about a missing preacher."

"A missing preacher?"

"Yep. He said they had a visiting preacher down here from Dallas for a meeting at his church yesterday evening. Said he and his pilot friend took off from the airstrip at Texas Pulp and Paper afterward, sometime around ten o'clock or so last night, headed back to Dallas. Now he says someone called him from Dallas and says they never made it home. Y'all had any reports up there about planes going down?"

"Just a minute and let me put you on with the sheriff," the dispatcher said.

A moment later, Sheriff Ray was on the phone, taking down as many details as he could. "Did they file a flight plan?" Ray asked.

"Not so far as I know. The pastor told me they weren't originally planning to leave last night but they got a report from the weather service about some fog that was supposed to be rolling in this morning, so they took off early. He says one of his deacons drove 'em to the air strip and watched 'em take off, then he shut down the lights. I don't know for sure what direction they would have headed, but if I just eyeball a map, looks to me like the most direct route would be over the Thicket up along your way. But I'm calling every county around to let 'em know."

"You got any kind of search organized yet?"

"Not yet, no, sir. Just making calls right now. I'm hoping somebody'll know something, like maybe these ol' boys made a forced landing somewhere, so no need for a search just yet."

"Seems like if they did, they would have called home."

"Yeah, I thought about that. Right now I'm just fishing to see if anyone heard anything that might help us pinpoint a search."

"I'll go ahead and get a search going. If they headed up this way, makes sense for me to get the ball rolling up here right now."

After getting the appropriate phone numbers for notifications if necessary and hanging up, Sheriff Ray followed up with a call to the Beaumont squadron of the Civil Air Patrol to see if he could get planes in the air. He knew the fellow that ran things down there, so he felt sure he could prevail upon him to commence a search even with no more information than they had.

The CAP, as a concept, originated in the late 1930s before its official founding in December of 1941. The idea was to utilize civilian pilots in World War II, rather than ground them, to aid in the war effort on the home front. CAP members were actually involved in patrolling for German U-boats along the U.S. coast and were even involved in dropping bombs and depth charges to deter the enemy. In 1948, the CAP officially became an auxiliary unit to the U.S. Air Force, not for combat purposes, but for benevolent purposes. That included, among other things, to aid in searches of exactly this nature.

Unfortunately, the remaining sunlight dictated that an air search would be delayed until the next morning. Then, three planes would be launched, sweeping the Big Thicket from above, searching for the missing pilot and preacher. In the meantime, radio reports went out on local stations that night in southeast Texas, hoping that someone might have heard or seen something Tuesday night. It was a long shot, but long shots were better than no shots.

CHAPTER EIGHTEEN

January 14, 1965

I didn't know if it was because hopelessness was beginning to set in, but the second night and going into the next morning seemed darker than the first. I was probably numb from the shock of the crash, but the night before I had an optimism that somebody had heard us go down and it would be just a matter of time before a search party would set out. My rational mind knew that wasn't the case. Even my initial discussions with Gabe, while he was still alive, confirmed that he had not filed a flight plan, so no one would have any reason to know that our plane was down until the day after we had taken off, at the earliest.

The second night also seemed colder. I no longer had the warmth, pitiful though it was, of burning sermon notes in my briefcase, nor the ability, if I chose, to seek refuge from wind inside the wreckage. Although I had not done so the night before, the fact that the fuselage was right there looming as an option gave some comfort that I could crawl inside it, if necessary, comfort that was now hours away, even if only a couple hundred yards. At least I had Gabe's jacket to provide some level of warmth.

Gabe. I hadn't seen him in a while.

Where had he gone this time? It had been hours since he disappeared again, as seemed to be his practice. I was still having a hard time figuring out what rules applied to him, be he ghost, angel, or hallucination. By now, though, I had become somewhat accustomed to his comings and goings that I was starting to equate with mood swings. Like maybe when he had reached his fill of me, he left, only to return later to poke and prod at my psyche again. Probably not fair of me to think that but trying to gauge the conduct of a ghost/hallucination/angel was new to me. This was, after all, my first experience with one of his ilk, whatever he was, and he didn't come with an instruction booklet.

I knew there was no point in trying to crawl after the meager sunlight disappeared a few hours ago. It had been hard enough during the day to see where I was going, snaking along at ground level in deep shadows, but nighttime was pitch black. Darker than Asashio's eyebrows times ten.

I still wasn't all that hungry, but I was parched with thirst. I figured the odds of finding any other source of water, buried or not, were pretty low. I also knew I needed to get some rest. Crawling for an entire day was task enough for someone who spent most of his days at a desk, or standing behind a pulpit, even if of sound body, but my strength and energy were both sapped by my injuries. I was completely spent, physically.

I tried to sleep on my side but needed my legs to keep me balanced in that position, a task I found impossible. I couldn't even bend my knees and tuck my legs upward. I simply had no control over them at all. They were nothing more than dead weight. Finally, I took off the backpack and, lying flat on my back, tucked it underneath my head, using a portion to cushion my neck. Not the best pillow I had ever found, but adequate under the circumstances. It wasn't like I could call room service.

Lying there, I thought about Juanita and the kids back in Duncanville. I figured that by now she knew we were missing, and she must be worried to death. The thought of her sitting at home with the kids, trying to calm and comfort them when she needed someone to calm and comfort her, made me angry at my predicament. Not angry at God, just at my predicament. I kept going back over things in my mind, the discussions I'd had with Gabe. Was I really a Jonah? Because if I was, I had no one to blame but myself.

But if I wasn't, did that mean God was to blame?

I was afraid I wouldn't be able to sleep, something I

desperately needed to replenish my depleted stock of energy, but before I knew it, exhaustion did its job and I slept. Or I blacked out. I wasn't sure which. Either way, it was a blessing. My sleep could be best described as restless, if you wanted to be generous. Even in my unconscious state, I was vaguely aware of intermittent slashes of hot pain tracking through my back and shooting down my legs, awakening me periodically. I actually welcomed that because I thought that, if I could feel pain in my legs, there was at least feeling. Pain was better than nothing, and I wondered if it meant there was hope of regaining full sensation. I didn't know if that was medically or scientifically sound thinking, but in bad circumstances, you had the option of conditioning yourself to either the worst or the best hope. I opted for the best.

After each of those slashes that awakened me, I was able to go back to sleep. Or black out, again. It seemed, though, as if my sleep was shallower each time. The last time I awoke, though, it was a noise that did it. Proof that my sleep was getting lighter. My first thought was that Gabe had returned to either watch over me or, more likely, to chastise me for sleeping when I should have been crawling.

I opened my eyes, but I couldn't see anything but Asashio's eyebrows. No moon, or if there was, it was blotted out by thick clouds.

I heard it again. It sounded close, yet I couldn't really tell for sure, any more than I could gauge how far off the highway was, since sound carried well on the still night air.

"Gabe? That you?"

I heard the sound again. Definitely nearby, close to my head. I rolled onto my stomach, raised up on my elbows, and peered into the darkness. Pitch black. That eyebrows thing.

Then something began to take shape not too far off.

I thought it was an optical illusion, at first. It looked like a faint light in the distance, moving back and forth. It gave the impression of someone swinging a lantern, or maybe a flashlight, back and forth. Searching for something. I couldn't see a hand or arm attached, but the only logical explanation was that a person was in control of that light. Something about that tickled my memory.

I retrieved the flashlight from my backpack and turned it on. I leaned on one arm, tilting my body to the side, and raised the flashlight in my other hand and aimed its beam toward the light in the distance. If I could see him or her—or it—surely whatever or whoever it was could see me, or at least see my light. If I could just attract attention.

"Over here!" I yelled.

My voice was weak, my mouth and throat dry, and the words came out as barely more than a whisper. Sound might carry on the night air, but it needed to be something deserving of the word "sound" first. I tried to salivate but gained nothing. I tried again, and this time a tiny bit of fluid seemed to materialize in the back of my mouth. I swallowed it, hoping to coat my throat at least some.

I yelled again.

"Hello! Hey, over here!" A little louder this time.

The light continued to swing back and forth but didn't appear to be drawing any closer. I stretched to raise my own light as high as I could, hoping its beam was visible to whoever was out there. Surely it was a search party, looking for me. It had to be looking for me. Why else would anyone be out here in the middle of the night?

"It's the ghost light," a voice said.

Gabe.

"It's the what?" I lowered my arm to the ground and released the flashlight, giving my forearm a rest.

"The ghost light. It's got several names, actually. The Bragg Light or the Saratoga Light."

Ahh, yes. I had heard of the Bragg Road Ghost Light, or the

Light of Saratoga, and knew just a tiny bit about them, but those were just legends. Weren't they?

"There used to be an old railroad line that ran between Bragg Station to Saratoga," Gabe said. It appeared that he deemed it necessary to lecture me on facts of the Big Thicket, his apparent new home for eternity. "The railroad line's gone now, but the bed for the line is still there and it makes a sort of road through some of the densest areas of the Thicket."

"So, tell me, are these like the Marfa Lights out in west Texas?"

The Marfa Lights, which were also sometimes called the Marfa ghost lights, could supposedly be seen east of Marfa, Texas, along the highway between Marfa and Presidio. There were various explanations for the lights, including supposition that they were nothing more than reflections of car lights along the highway or that they were some unexplained atmospheric phenomenon.

But what I was seeing right then were real live, bona fide lights. Not legends. Not atmospheric phenomena, not on the floor of a forest. But maybe traffic lights from that highway I kept hearing.

"Most of the explanations for these lights are not nearly as benign as the ones in Marfa," Gabe said. "For the romantic, there's the notion that the lights mark the location of treasure buried by Spanish Conquistadors. If that's true, might be worth you crawling over that way and digging, like you did at that ol' stump. Might make you a rich man."

"Lot of good that does me if I don't make it out of here."

"Then there's the story that it's the remains of a fire started by a Confederate officer to smoke out Yankees during the Civil War. Some think it's a guy who got lost hunting at night and he's doomed to spend the rest of eternity carrying a torch while trying to find a way out.

"Then there's my personal favorite. A railroad worker was

decapitated in a train wreck and he spends his nights looking for his head."

"I've heard that one before, too. Just a legend. A ghost story."

"Look at me," Gabe said. "Aren't I enough to make you believe in ghosts?"

"So, are you saying you are a ghost?"

Gabe laughed. "Truth is, I don't really know. But just in case, if you crawl across a decapitated head while you're wallowing around out here, sing out."

He laughed again at his own dark humor.

"Not funny," I said.

"Preacher, might as well laugh or else you'll cry."

"How do you know all this stuff?" I asked. "Being a native Texan, I've heard some of the legends, at least the broad strokes, but you sure seem to know a lot more of the facts. Since when did you become a Big Thicket historian?"

Gabe crossed his arms over his chest and blew a puff of air between his lips, as if thinking about the question. After a brief moment, he said, "I don't know. I guess maybe the dead get some kind of inspiration or insight into the places where they died."

"Well, let me ask you this. You don't seem to know exactly what you are, but doesn't it make sense that, if you're a ghost, you ought to be able to see other ghosts?"

Gabe thought about the question, then shook his head. "I suppose that makes sense, but like I said, I haven't figured out the rules yet."

Suddenly a scream pierced the night air. High-pitched, like a banshee, a spirit whose wail signaled impending death. Bone chilling. And nearby. A shiver ran down my spine, and even seemed to traverse the sciatic nerve to my legs. If it really was a banshee, whose death did it portend?

Gabe was already dead so, unless there was someone else

nearby crawling around on the floor of the Thicket, it could only mean me.

Another scream, just as loud. But less of a wail this time, and more of a genuine scream. A woman's scream.

"That was real," I said. "Someone's in trouble out there."

"And you're not?"

I grabbed the flashlight again and waved it overhead. Maybe she could see my light. I wasn't going to be able to go to her, but maybe she could come to me. I didn't know how much help I could be, groveling in the dead leaves, but maybe there was strength to be found in numbers. Or maybe, just maybe, she knew the way out and could go for help.

Then again, if she knew an escape route, why was she out there screaming? What if, instead of being in trouble, she was some kind of crazy woman? What if she didn't need help, but instead she posed a threat?

I decided that it wasn't much of a choice to make. I didn't think I could be much worse off than I already was, and the odds said her scream was a cry for help.

I decided I would offer whatever help I could.

"Over here!" I yelled. The urgency of her scream had brought the return of my full voice, dry as my throat was. Adrenaline, I supposed.

"You sure you want her to hear you?" Gabe asked.

"She needs help."

"What kind of help do you plan to give her?"

Good question, one I had already considered. But I figured that was a problem for later. Like I really needed more problems.

The woman screamed again. The sound seemed to split the night. High-pitched, like she was screaming at the top of her lungs.

But this time, when it tailed off and died out, it ended with a guttural moan. A deep, throaty sound that seemed inconsistent with the high-pitch scream that preceded it.

A growl.

The growl seemed to go on forever. My blood ran cold. I felt a tingling sensation in my legs again. I tried to move them, to pull them up underneath me to allow me to move on hands and knees, but I couldn't. They tingled painfully as if the nerve endings were attached to a car battery. Sensation without control. Pain without relief.

I heard movement in the underbrush. It sounded like something thrashing around on the dried leaves that littered the floor of the forest. Whatever it was, it seemed to be getting closer.

A scream again. Even closer this time. It seemed to have found me and was homing in.

"I told you about the panthers before, preacher," Gabe said.

I lowered the flashlight and turned it off. If that was a panther, no need to light a path for it.

"You think that's a panther?" I asked.

"I can assure you it's not a poor woman out here all alone."

"Do you think it heard me?"

"Doesn't matter if it can. It can smell blood." He paused then added, "Your blood."

I remembered pain in my forehead when we crashed, but I had felt no blood when I checked it. I put my hand to my face and brought it down, then briefly illuminated it with the flashlight's beam. Nothing.

"I'm not bleeding," I said.

"You're too literal. I was speaking figuratively, preacher. Blood is just a euphemism for scent. It's the human scent he smells. Yours."

"Maybe it's you," I said. "Maybe he smells the dead."

"You willing to take that chance?"

I tucked the flashlight back into the backpack and lay as still as I could. My mind tried to formulate a plan of action, but all I could think to do was hope the panther couldn't really smell me, at least not distinctly enough to make out exactly where I was. And I hoped there were other scents of animals in the woods that might throw him off. Maybe it really was the smell of death that attracted him. If so, Gabe could disappear again, or head off in another direction. I hoped it would fake the animal out and draw it away. But hope wasn't much of a plan. I also knew it was false hope.

I had to move.

"What are you going to do?" Gabe asked.

"I don't know, but I'm open to suggestions."

"Isn't this the time when you say you'll pray about it and wait for God to deliver you?"

"Don't underestimate the power of prayer."

"Did you hear the one about the bear chasing the Christian in the woods?"

"I don't believe I know that one."

"There's this Christian in the forest and a big ol' bear is after him. The Christian is running just as fast as he can, but he figures out pretty quick he can't outrun the bear. So what does he do? Why, what all good Christians would do. He drops right down on his knees and starts praying.

"After a few minutes, he realizes the bear has caught up to him but hasn't made any effort to gobble him up. So he opens his eyes and looks back at the bear. And lo and behold, would you believe it, that ol' bear is kneeling, too. He's got his paws together in front of him and he's moving his lips like he's praying.

"So the Christian says, 'Lord, thank you for making this a God-fearing Christian bear.' Then he realizes that he can understand what the bear is saying."

Gabe paused before getting to the punch line. I waited for it.

"The bear is saying, 'Thank you for this food which we are about to eat.'"

Then he laughed, as if he had just told the world's funniest joke.

"Good one," I said "But I wouldn't quit your day job."

"Riddle me this, preacher," Gabe said. "What good is prayer now? Where's God now?"

"Like I said, don't underestimate the power of prayer. But remember, it's not just about prayer. It's about faith, and it's about action. Putting feet to your prayers. After you get down on your knees, then you get up on your feet and get going."

"I think you're gonna have to rule out that feet thing, aren't you?" he asked. Then, abruptly, he disappeared.

I shook my head and tried to tune him out but he had a point. My entire ministry, brief as it had been, I had heard people criticize Christians for relying solely on "thoughts and prayers" when circumstances called for action. There was nothing wrong with thoughts and prayers, but God expected us as his people to back up those prayers. He even told us, in James 2:17, that faith without works is dead. And right then, I needed to put action to my prayers even if couldn't put feet to them.

I had to get out of there. Any way I could.

I closed my eyes and listened. Concentrated hard. I could again hear faint sounds in the distance. But this time they weren't screams or growls. Nothing thrashing around in dead leaves. It was the same thing I had heard that first night, lying by the wreckage of the plane. Traffic noise. How far away, I couldn't tell. But I could detect the direction from which the noise came and, thankfully, it appeared to be the opposite direction from the big cat.

I slung the backpack over my shoulders and crawled, face down, elbows digging into the ground and pulling myself forward. In the direction of some distant, but very real, highway.

CHAPTER NINETEEN

Behind me, the rustling in the undergrowth seemed to do no more than keep pace with my snail's crawl. I wasn't extending my lead, nor did the panther, if indeed that was what it was, seem to be gaining on me. That was hard to believe, given my glacial movement, but maybe it was just toying with me. Like a cat playing with the proverbial mouse, and I was the mouse. It was hard to tell how far behind me it was.

The way sound traveled at night in the woods, it could have been as much as a quarter of a mile or it could have been fifty yards. But trying to make that determination was purely a theoretical exercise. The pertinent truth was that, so long as it didn't gain ground, the distance didn't really matter. I was content to keep going as long as there was a gap between us.

Then I heard rustling of leaves right at my left shoulder. I hadn't heard the panther close the gap, so it startled me. Was this yet another predator in the woods?

I kept moving forward, such as it was. I glanced to my left. I saw a booted foot. I felt a jolt of hope. A rescuer from a search party. But no, I recognized that boot.

Gabe. Good ol' here again, gone again, taunt-you-while-I'm here again Gabe.

"I gotta give it to you, preacher man, you got guts," he said. "When you said you don't quit, maybe you did mean it after all. Of course, that ol' cat's just playing with you. When he gets hungry enough, this'll all be over. Fast."

I kept crawling, ignoring his jibe. He walked beside me, taking baby steps to stay back with me. Leaves rustled with each step he took. Should that be the way it happened? Shouldn't a ghost just sorta hover above the ground? Shouldn't an angel? But a hallucination . . . well, I supposed that was a different story. If I could hallucinate Gabe, why couldn't I hallucinate the sounds of his footsteps, too?

He walked around in front of me and squatted, facing me. "What's the matter? Cat got your tongue?" He laughed. "Well, not yet I guess." Now he was just being mean.

I ignored him still. I dug in an elbow and pulled myself forward, straight at him. I'd either go right through him or he'd have to move.

He moved. He straightened and walked alongside me again. "Come on, preacher, don't get sore at me," he said. "Just trying to make conversation."

"Is that what you call it?" I asked. "I thought conversation was a give and take exchange of thoughts and ideas, not a one-sided assault of sarcasm and discouragement."

"There you go. Good. You're mad. Just wanted to make sure you were still with me."

"You'll understand if I don't have either the time or the inclination to carry on this so-called conversation right now."

Even in the chill of the night, I was perspiring. Heavily. Sweat rolled along the sides of my face, trickled across the back of my neck as it traversed from my scalp down my back. I felt beads gather at my brow, threatening to drop into my eyes and blind me. That seemed like a ridiculous worry since I was dealing with Asashio's eyebrows to start with. Still, I rubbed my forearm across my face to brush the sweat away.

And when I looked forward again, I saw lights. Not swinging lights, like the ghost lantern—or whatever it was—I had seen earlier. Nor was it a steady light, like a house fixture. Nor was it distinct. Instead, it was more like light*ness* as opposed to a specific light. A brightening of some sort.

And then it disappeared.

Vehicular traffic? Maybe. A car's or truck's headlights briefly illuminating the highway and then the vehicle moved on past. But that meant I was right. There, in fact, was a roadway of some sort nearby. And even in the black of night, it was being traversed by human beings in motorized vehicles.

Those thoughts motivated me to greater effort. If I could reach the highway, surely another vehicle would be by at some point. And surely its headlights would capture the form of a man on the side of the road waving a white shirt overhead.

Another bit of lightness appeared, grew stronger, then disappeared, this time accompanied by tell-tale sounds of a large truck engine.

Gabe pointed ahead. It wasn't just a hallucination. Apparently, he saw the same thing I did.

"See that, preacher?" he asked. There was even an excited tone in his voice, a welcome relief from sarcasm. "You were right. There's a highway up ahead. Think you can get there before that cat gets to you?"

As if to emphasize the point, the panther screamed again. But this time, I could tell he had made up some ground on me. This time, it sounded close. Unlike before, this time I could almost feel the disturbance in the night air caused by sound waves from the scream. Fifty yards away, maybe. Maybe closer. My window of opportunity for escape was closing. Fast.

I dug hard and deep, as if by burying my elbows into the loose leaves and dirt were the equivalent of pressing down harder on a car accelerator. It didn't actually propel me any farther or faster with each stroke, but it gave me the sense that I was doing something sufficient to improve my lot. I refused to allow my rational mind to disabuse me of that notion.

I wasn't sure how long I crawled after seeing those traffic lights—again, it seemed like hours but was probably more like ten or fifteen minutes—when I reached another fallen tree. I couldn't see it but when I reached a hand forward for my next elbow of sod, my fingertips crashed into the rough bark.

I could still hear the cat moving through the underbrush behind me. Toward me. It moved silently, except for the occasional crunch of leaves. And a soft, almost purring sound, like a large housecat. The kind that might curl up on a windowsill and sleep in the sun. But I knew there was nothing tame or domesticated about my stalker. And there was no windowsill or warming sun.

"What are you gonna do, preacher?" Gabe asked.

He sat astraddle the trunk of the tree, like a cowboy on a horse, arms folded across his chest, and looked down at me.

"I don't think you've got time to crawl around this one," he said. "You can't tell in the dark, but I can. It's a good twenty feet in either direction to reach the opposite ends. How long will that take you? And I'd hate for you to have to start from scratch to dig your way under it. There's not a depression already started for you like the last time. So, what are you going to do?"

Good question. At my rate of speed, it would take me a good five minutes or so to reach the ends to go around. And digging was an even worse option.

I reached upward to see how tall the tree was lying horizontally on the ground. I placed my palm against the bark and worked my hand upward with stair-stepping fingers. If I strained, I could place my hand fully on top of the tree. That told me it wasn't too big, probably only about three feet in diameter. I realized I had but one real option, and even that might not be possible if the panther kept gaining on me as it had.

But the sounds of rustling leaves had stopped, as if the cat had stopped, as well. Waiting, but for what?

I removed the backpack from my shoulders. It didn't contain much, just a few meager possessions, but it had become somewhat of a security blanket for me. Besides serving as my pillow, it also contained the flashlight, which well might be needed in the dark, and the white shirt for waving. If only I got a chance to wave it.

With one swing, I tossed it over the log, as if shooting a basketball hook shot. I heard it land in a pile of dry leaves on the other side.

I got on one elbow and reached up with the other hand until, again, my palm lay flat on the top of the rounded trunk. I squeezed my fingers and gripped it tightly to brace my upper body, then reached with my other hand and found similar purchase against the rough timber. Both hands now grasped the top of the trunk. Though exhausted, my arms screaming to rest, I pulled. It was like doing a most awkward pull-up. Instead of raising my legs beneath me, as in a conventional pull-up, they dragged along the ground, creating nearly insurmountable friction. It seemed as if I made no progress. Hanging there, exposed, I said a silent prayer to a God I almost felt had deserted me. *Almost.* Not a prayer for deliverance, but a prayer for strength.

Then, suddenly, I began to feel a flow of energy. As if in one brief moment, God had infused me with his strength. It must have been how Samson felt when, shorn of his hair and his strength, God restored his power to enable him to bring down the great hall in Gaza to destroy his enemy, the Philistines. Would God grant me the strength to destroy the stalking panther?

I managed to raise my torso off the ground until my chest pressed against the side of the tree. Utilizing a swimming motion, I worked my hands farther along and over the rounded trunk, pulling myself up and up. Just when I thought I was going to have to let go and drop back down, I found that my chest was starting to round the curve at the top of the trunk. My useless legs were still dead weight behind me, but I kept pulling with arms that, miraculously, seemed endowed with a strength I had never felt even in the vigor of my youth. I knew it wasn't my strength, but God-given strength. And, if that was the case, it fueled a belief that my time had not yet come, that God was not finished with me.

"Go, preacher man, go," Gabe said. He no longer sat astride the tree but had gotten off on the far side. He leaned on his fists on the tree and watched me. "If I wasn't seeing it with my own eyes, I wouldn't believe it."

Inch by inch, I pulled myself upward. Upward. Then I began working my way over.

When my chest rested on top of the tree, I reached downward and could feel the ground on the other side. I wriggled my way across the trunk until my head reached the other side, then my chest, with my head now downward. When I got my upper body forward far enough, the weight of my torso carried me the rest of the way to the ground on the other side. I braced my fall with my hands and arms, tucked my head, and flipped over to the ground.

I rolled onto my back and lay there. I wiped sweat from my face. Perspiration soaked my shirt and suit coat beneath Gabe's flight jacket. My hair was as damp as if I had just gotten out of a shower, creating a chill in the January night air.

Gabe turned his back to the tree and sat down. "You know, I'd say congratulations, but the game's not over yet."

I looked up at him. I could barely see his face in the darkness, even though it was just a few feet above me. I mostly just made out the outline of his head and could see the white of his teeth when he spoke again.

"That ol' cat won't have nearly as much trouble as you did clearing this tree."

As soon as the words came out of his mouth, the panther screamed. I couldn't tell how close it was, but it sounded like no more than twenty or thirty yards. Ground it could easily cover, a gap it could easily close, in just a few leaps.

I rolled back onto my chest and looked forward, but I couldn't see anything. No more lights. I listened but heard nothing. No traffic sounds. Seemed like an awfully big gap in traffic. Then again, this time of night on a country highway, it made sense that traffic would be light, with huge gaps of time between the passing of cars.

Or could it be that I had been hallucinating? I supposed it

certainly could have been, just like I was hallucinating Gabe. Still, I had to act as if it were real.

So, I began to crawl again. I got no more than a few feet when I reached forward and hit metal. Chain link. A chain link fence, old and rusted though it might be, that completely blocked my way. I extracted the flashlight from my backpack and shined the light on it. At least four feet tall, topped with barbed wire. The fence meant someone had been around here and thought enough to block off some area with fencing. Maybe it was even close enough to the highway that it was intended for traffic safety. But, from the looks of the rust covering the links and the way it sagged, building it was ancient history.

As I lay there, I realized that I was enclosed in a prison created by a tree trunk on one side and a fence on the other, with no way out. I was simply a meal waiting for the panther to arrive.

"Bummer," Gabe said. "Boy, that God's a funny guy, isn't he?"

Again, I wasn't sure if Gabe's job was to motivate me or simply to discourage me, but it sure seemed more like the latter than the former.

I began to laugh. Just a chuckle at first, then bigger and louder. Uncontrollably. There was nothing funny about it, and the hopelessness of my situation pressed down on my spirits.

After a while, I was just about laughed out. I lay there, silently, waiting for the panther to make its move. But strangely, it did nothing.

"Maybe it feels sorry for you," Gabe said.

"Maybe. It doesn't seem like there's much else I can do except wait for it."

"Tell you what," Gabe said. "Let's change the subject and see if we can pass the time. Who knows, maybe the cat'll get bored and go away."

That sounded like as good a plan as any I could come up

with. Except maybe to use the flashlight as a club and beat the panther over the head with it when it finally attacked.

"Or maybe," Gabe said, "we can figure out why you're in this predicament and see if God's got a way out for you. So let's start with how you ended up back in Texas?"

There he was again, prodding me to search my heart. More evidence that maybe he was more than just a ghost or hallucination. So, I again considered the choices in my life that had led me to this point and laid them out for Gabe.

CHAPTER TWENTY

When I was a student at New Orleans Baptist Theological Seminary, I spent some time working for Dr. Gray Allison, who was on the faculty. He taught Missions Evangelism, as part of a faculty mission program, and I was in his class. Though I had spent time in Japan as part of those mission trips while I was at Baylor, it was Dr. Allison's class that first really tugged at my heart strings about the possibility of being a full-time missionary in a foreign land. I knew that such a decision would require a lot of prayer and would also require Juanita's agreement. After all, picking up your immediate family and moving to a country far away from grandparents, aunts, uncles, and cousins, with all the love and support they provided to you and your kids – and I had two young children to think about – was not a decision to be made rashly. Nor was it a decision to be made simply because you "thought" it was God's will for your life. It was something you needed to be sure of.

Dr. John Abernathy was one of our Southern Baptist missionaries, who had been imprisoned in a Japanese prison camp following the attack on Pearl Harbor. After that, he served in Korea following the Korean War and the withdrawal of the Chinese. I was lucky enough that he visited the campus during my time there because I was working on a research paper on the role of revival in the modern missionary enterprise, and he would be a great resource for my studies. I was focused not just on mission work broadly, but specifically on religious revivalism, which I had seen defined as involving periodic movements of intense spiritual upheaval and awakening.

Our own country had a history of such revivals, including what had become known as "The Great Awakening," which started under the pastorate of a young Jonathan Edwards in Northampton, Massachusetts. It stretched from 1734 to 1743. Another, sometimes referred to as "The Second Great

Awakening," broke out in 1800 in Logan County, Kentucky, and culminated in the Cane Ridge Revival, with as many as 20,000 attendees of various protestant denominations, including Presbyterian, Baptist, and Methodist. Some scholars said it lasted until 1840.

Other, more well-known such revivals included The Urban Revivals in Chicago from 1875 to 1885, in which Dwight L. Moody, who forsook pursuing a fortune as a shoe salesman for a life of service as an evangelist, participated, and the Welsh Revivals of the early 1900s that started among Welsh-speaking residents of Pennsylvania and spread as far away as Michigan and Ohio, and even to South Carolina and Georgia in the south. A key figure in those revivals was Billy Sunday, a former professional baseball player who converted to Christianity and left baseball for an evangelistic ministry, becoming one of the best-known evangelists of his time.

As part of my research, I had read a short book of scarcely more than 100 pages authored by Mary K. Crawford called *The Shantung Revival*, which had been published in Shanghai in 1933. The book was primarily a compilation of testimonies of people who had been involved in a revival in Shantung Province in northern China that started in 1927 in the village of Chefoo and ultimately continued until roughly 1937, with its zenith occurring in 1932 and 1933. It was centered primarily in areas ministered to by Southern Baptist missionaries. Crawford disclaimed any authorship of the book since she was, according to her own account, merely a "compiler" of those testimonies and "there is almost no original composition in it." Instead, she said, it was "composed of letters and testimonies written informally as friend to friend . . . written that Jesus Christ might be glorified."

It seemed like it took me an unreasonably long time to read such a short book. I could devour tomes that were hundreds of pages in length, but this one grabbed hold of me like few I had come across before. I found that, as I read, I had to stop from time to time to pray for a little while, then to cry for a little while, then go back and read some more. As a result, it had a tremendous impact on my life.

Dr. Allison knew about my interest in mission work, as well as about my research and my reading the book. He also knew that Dr. Abernathy had been involved in that revival in China. So, he made an appointment for the two of us to meet with Dr. Abernathy to talk about missions, in general, but the Shantung Revival, in particular.

Sitting down with Dr. Abernathy, I heard, for the first time, somebody talk about the unusual events of such a revival, including scores of people being "filled" with the Holy Spirit. As Ms. Crawford recorded it in one of the testimonies she compiled, from a Chinese man who said that he "will surrender it all" to the Lord: "Then it seemed that there were magnets all around me pulling everything in me out. I realized that the Lord was cleansing me, and I was saying, 'All gone.' After that for ten or fifteen minutes I was resting, it seemed to me in the very arms of Jesus. It came to me all of a sudden that I had gotten Jesus. I was literally lost in Him and He in me."

Now, being a good ol' Southern Baptist, the notion of being filled with the Holy Spirit – with the accompanying histrionics, a term I use in the literal sense, meaning overly dramatic or emotional, and not pejoratively – was something we relegated to the charismatic denominations that might have bought more literally into the story of believers being spirit-filled during Pentecost. Speaking in tongues and falling and rolling on the ground and healing of infirmities and other things of that nature were foreign to me. Those were events I had never witnessed, and certainly never participated in, which left me with a hefty dose of skepticism. But as I listened to Dr. Abernathy, I realized that what I might term histrionics were things he had personally witnessed and that he genuinely believed them to be God-sent and real. So, who was I, who hadn't been there, to question someone who had?

In the aftermath of that meeting, I first began to develop, for want of a better description, what I called a sense of "divine appointment." I realized that for many Christians, terming something as being God's "call" was just a way to legitimize what they already wanted to do. But this was different. This was real. Even though I was interested in missionary work, I couldn't say I yearned or desired to do so. But the stories I heard opened my mind to something new.

And because of my service in Japan while in the Army, and subsequent mission trips there while at Baylor, I felt that sense of appointment naturally directing me to Japan. I wondered if, perhaps, it was my destiny to be involved in a revival in Japan similar to that in Shantung Province.

Later, while I was on the mission field in Japan, first in Tokyo and later in Sapporo, that thought was stimulated in my mind from time to time. It was a heady feeling, believing that God might have appointed me to lead, or at least participate in, such a revival. One day, I had the chance to meet with a missionary couple passing through Tokyo on their way home to the States after retiring from their service in Korea. As we talked, they informed me that they had been in Shantung Province at the time of the revival which, at that point, was close to 30 years in the past. The most significant thing that came out of that conversation, something I'll never forget, is when the husband told me: "It would be a tragedy to go to the mission field and have to come home and never see something like that."

While serving in Japan, I'd had the opportunity to make a mission trip to Taiwan, a relatively short hop from Japan— shorter than from Dallas to New York—where I first met Dr. C.L. "Charlie" Culpepper, who had also been at Shantung. Charlie had been born in my native Texas, between San Antonio and Houston in Lavaca County, and he got his B.A. from my alma mater Baylor University in 1919, before obtaining both his master and doctorate degrees in theology from Southwestern Baptist Theological Seminary in Fort Worth. In 1923, he had been appointed by the Foreign Mission Board as a missionary to China, where he served until the communist takeover of that country in 1949.

With both of us being Texans, we naturally struck up a friendship. I spoke at length with him about the Shantung Revival, and I recall sitting with him on the side of Grass Mountain, overlooking the city of Taipei, until about four a.m. one morning, listening to him talk about it. As with Dr. Abernathy when I met with him at the seminary, here was a man who had witnessed things that were hard to believe, but who assured me that they had been real and they had actually happened. He expressed his desire that other places, including the United States, would experience the same.

About a year later, I made a mission trip to the Philippines, where I spoke at a meeting that took place in Philippine Baptist Seminary in the Guisad Valley in Baguio City. The seminary was relatively new at the time, having been established in 1951 under the leadership of Dr. Frank P. Lide, who first went to China as a missionary in 1920, and was still serving there when World War II broke out. He was imprisoned by the Japanese for a time before being exchanged and returned home in 1943.

I met with Dr. Lide, who it turned out had also been in Shantung Province during the period of revival. It seemed as if everywhere I turned, I was running head-on into the Shantung Revival. Hard to believe it could simply be coincidence. Surely, God was reaffirming that sense of divine appointment that I felt. I listened to Dr. Lide tell the same kind of stories, the same first-hand accounts, about the revival as had Dr. Culpepper and Dr. Abernathy.

Man, I thought, *if I could just be a part of something like that in Japan.*

It reinforced my belief that perhaps something like this was what that divine sense of appointment was all about. I again asked myself whether I was meant to be involved in, or maybe even lead, a spiritual awakening in post-war Japan like had happened in Shantung. But up until then, after having been in Japan for a few years, nothing even remotely like the Shantung Revival had occurred.

Oh, sure, I had helped orchestrate what we called the Japan Baptist New Life Movement in Tokyo, a series of evangelistic meetings jointly sponsored by the Baptist General Convention of Texas, the Southern Baptist Convention Foreign Mission Board, and the Japan Baptist Convention. And I helped Japanese pastors and lay workers start and develop churches across the country, and taught them how to extend their evangelistic outreach, which included conducting monthly seminars for pastors.

Juanita had also been heavily involved. She had started and taught Sunday school classes at Sapporo Baptist Church, worked with the Woman's Missionary Society, and also served as a representative to Hokkaido for the Japan Woman's Missionary Union. But despite all that effort, and despite making serious evangelistic inroads in a country that was massively non-Christian, I couldn't see any equivalent to the Shantung Revival on the horizon.

In 1963, as we neared the end of our five-year term in Japan, it became clear that there was not going to be a revival like that in Japan. At least not while I was there. I was by disposition very optimistic in outlook—something, I might add, that was being tested mightily in the Big Thicket—but for the first time I began to have periods of depression. I didn't believe there was anything organic to it, nothing that could be treated with pharmaceuticals. Rather, it was a spiritual and emotional depression. I knew the root of it. It was caused by the nagging question: Was it possible that I had come to Japan, and been in the right place at the right time for a spiritual revival, but I had missed that divine appointment? Could it be that I was not in the right spiritual condition or that, if I was, had simply missed it? Or could it be that I had failed in my responsibility to be an instrument of that revival and the failure of it to materialize had been my fault?

That raised a terrible follow-up question: Even having not yet reached the age of 40, had I lived past the real purpose for my life? What a tragedy, that missionary husband had said, to go to the mission field and come home and never see something like the revival in Shantung. But I had been in Japan for five years, a full term, and hadn't seen anything like it.

So, when we left Japan on furlough, I began suffering serious depression about it. I knew, in hindsight, maybe I was just premature. After all, I had been in Japan for only five years. But Dr. Culpepper had been in China for less than that when the revival broke out. Maybe it wasn't fair to compare myself to him, but I did. I never mentioned my depression to anybody, not even Juanita. She could tell something was wrong, but she didn't press me on it. She figured, I supposed, that when I was ready to talk about it, I would.

As we left Japan to return to the States on furlough, now with three kids in tow, Stevie having been born in Kyoto in 1960, the Office of Press Relations issued a press release about me. I had to admit, I sounded pretty good on paper. That release said:

> Dr. Theron V. (Corky) Farris, Southern Baptist missionary to Japan, works with Baptist churches and missions on the island of Hokkaido, helping Japanese pastors and lay workers develop strong churches and extend their evangelistic outreach. His duties include conducting a monthly seminar for pastors, in which subjects such as evangelism and church programming are studied. He and his family

make their home in Sapporo, capital of Hokkaido Prefecture.

Dr. Farris was stationed in Sapporo after World War II as a member of the U.S. Army's occupational forces. He says that while in Japan he was primarily impressed by the country's natural beauty and postwar destitution of its people. After returning to the States he became disturbed about the spiritual condition of the Japanese and decided to go back as a missionary. Appointed by the Foreign Mission Board in 1957, he studied Japanese in Tokyo for two years before settling in Sapporo.

A native of Fort Worth, Tex., Dr. Farris attended Southern Methodist University, Dallas, Tex., and Texas Wesleyan College, Fort Worth, and graduated from Baylor University, Waco, Tex., with the Bachelor of Arts degree and from New Orleans (La.) Baptist Theological Seminary with the Bachelor of Divinity and Doctor of Theology degrees. While a college student he made three summer preaching trips to Japan.

At the time of his missionary appointment he was pastor of Osyka (Miss.) Baptist Church. Previously he pastored Goodwood Baptist Church, Baton Rouge, La., and Ninth Street Mission, Waco, and served as assistant to the director of mission work at New Orleans Seminary.

He and his wife, the former Juanita Peacock, of Fort Worth, have three children, Darlyne, Michael, and Stephen.

Dr. Farris expects to study at Johns Hopkins University, Baltimore, Md., during his furlough.

For our time of furlough, we located in the northeast, near Baltimore, so I could do some post-graduate work at Oriental Seminary at Johns Hopkins University. We at first lived in a rented house in a Baltimore suburb called Joppatowne. We had barely settled into our house in Joppatowne before I received a telegram from the chairman of the pulpit committee at First Baptist Church of Wrightstown, New Jersey, that said: "The First Baptist Church of Wrightstown under the leadership of the Holy Spirit tonight during our regular business sessions extends a call to you to be our interim pastor." After considerable prayer, I accepted the position for this small church whose congregation was largely composed of military families from nearby McGuire Air Force Base.

At first, our little family commuted to Wrightstown on weekends for church services, then we moved there to be closer to the church, while I commuted the 120 miles between there and Baltimore for my classes. Shortly before the furlough time was over, and we were preparing to return to Japan, I got a call out of the blue from an old friend, Dr. C. Wade Freeman, who was director of the Evangelism Division of the Baptist General Convention of Texas in Dallas.

"Corky," he said, "I would like to invite you to consider joining our staff here in Dallas at the Evangelism Division on a full-time basis."

He made it clear that this was not a firm offer, at least not yet. He told me that he would have to make a recommendation to the State Missions Board and possibly to the Executive Board of the Baptist General Convention of Texas, but before he made such a recommendation, he needed to know if I was interested. I understood, though, that the recommendation was more of a formality than anything, and that, once made, the deed was as good as done.

The invitation caught me completely off guard since, as I

said, I was already planning our family's return to Japan. I believed that God had been in the initial decision to go to Japan, having laid the groundwork years earlier with those student mission trips to Japan while I was at Baylor, not to mention my time of military service in that country. I didn't believe that my missionary work had reached its end, especially since I had not yet experienced my own version of the Shantung Revival. So, my initial reaction was to decline.

"I just don't see how on earth I could do that," I said.

"Well, I know this is sudden," he replied, "but before you decide, will you and your wife let us fly you down here to discuss the opportunity in person?" Then he added, "If the Lord doesn't confirm that it's the right thing for you to do, then that'll be fine."

That was an awful hard proposition to pass up, especially since it meant a free trip back home. What's more, it was imminently reasonable to ask us to personally see what the invitation actually entailed so that whatever decision I made, it would at least be an informed decision. So we took him up on it. We found someone to stay with the kids in New Jersey and prepared to return to Texas for the first time in several years. To be honest, I was more excited about that trip home than the job offer, which I still didn't see how I could seriously entertain.

After making the trip, as we were flying back to Baltimore, Juanita and I both felt that the move was the right thing to do.

"We've got to be real sure," I said to her, as we winged our way northeast. "We can't afford to make a mistake here, because that will burn a bridge with the Foreign Mission Board."

"I know."

"Besides, we've worked so hard for the language." I was referring to the couple of years of intensive Japanese language study in Tokyo for the both of us. Intensive enough that I had become fluent to the point of no longer needing interpreters when I preached.

"I know."

"We can't afford to jump up on one side of the horse and off on the other side." Trotting out my Texas metaphors. "And we can't afford to make a decision and then, three years later, realize we've made a mistake."

"I know." My patient longsuffering wife.

So we prayed about it and came to the clear conviction that God was directing us to move to Texas. Dr. Freeman submitted my name to the Mission Board and the Executive Commission and, acting on the unanimous decision of the Evangelism Division, on September 25, 1964, Dr. Freeman formally welcomed me aboard. In his letter, he wrote: "You are coming to one of the greatest opportunities in the Southern Baptist Convention, and God has made you more than equal to the demanding position. I think He has been preparing you across the years for all that should and must be done in leading our people to be witnesses for Him."

So, I thought, my Shantung Revival will come in Texas, not Japan.

"But it didn't take three years to start second-guessing the decision, like I warned Juanita," I said.

"I guess not," Gabe said. "It's barely been three months."

"I suppose if I had turned the position down, and we had gone back to Japan, everything would have been different. At least I wouldn't be lying here on the floor of the Big Thicket."

"For all you know, you'd be lying on the floor of some other forest, way over there in Japan."

"Maybe. But I've got to wonder if I'm lying here because I made a mistake. What if I just wanted to come back to Texas and God wanted me in Japan?"

"Do you think that's the case?"

I thought about it for a moment, then shook my head. "I don't know. But if he wanted me here, that raises a thought I'd really rather not think about right now."

I started laughing again, though I couldn't explain why. Maybe it was just the hopelessness of my situation. Or maybe it was exhaustion. Or maybe I was becoming delirious. But, as I was reminded, I'd rather laugh than cry.

***

One day while I was visiting the seminary in the Philippines, its founder Dr. Frank Lide asked me to join him at his home for lunch. I was thrilled to go and spend some time alone with him and to listen to him talk about the great revival in Shantung. I sat, rapt, almost unable to eat as I heard the stories he told of God's work in China, like those I had heard from others. I didn't have any questions to ask because I didn't want to interrupt the stream of his narrative.

After we finished our meal, he said, "Now, Brother Corky, before you go, why don't we have a word of prayer together."

I replied that I thought that would be great. So we went into a back bedroom in his house and we knelt on opposite sides of the bed. He invited me to pray first, which I did. And if I did say so myself, it was one of my finer prayers. I prayed around the world and back again, prayed for everything that I thought was a worthy prayer object, and then said my "amen." I guess it probably took, oh, about two, two and a half-minutes.

When I finished, Dr. Lide began to pray.

Now, I had thought he lived there in that house alone, but as he began to pray, I realized that someone else lived there, as well. God lived there. And when Dr. Lide began to talk to Him, it seemed as he was engaged in a conversation with someone right there in that room. I was tempted to open my eyes and look around to see who he was talking to. It was a genuine conversation with God, and Dr. Lide spoke as if only he and God were in the room.

And then he started to laugh.

It was as if the laughter started somewhere far away in a

cavern. Deep, echoing. It just came rumbling, rolling out. I had never heard anything like it before, nor since.

Then I recalled a story I had heard about one of the missionaries in Shantung Province who, following his experience of being filled with the Holy Spirit, would laugh when he prayed. The person telling the story had a descriptor for it: holy laughter. I realized that was the only way to describe what Dr. Lide was doing: holy laughter.

Lying on the ground on the floor of the Big Thicket, mine was not holy laughter. My laughs turned to sobs.

Gabe leaned over and looked at me. Even in the dark, I could clearly see his face. An expression on it said that even he couldn't bear the heartbreak of the moment.

So he faded away.

CHAPTER TWENTY-ONE

I tried to rally myself. Self-pity wasn't going to help, nor was now the time to quit. For all my on again, off again bravado with Gabe, including my "I never quit" story from basic training, the truth was that sometimes quitting was the best option. Continuing to do something for no other reason than you started it was not a meritorious decision. You didn't get a gold star for beating your head against a brick wall, then when you made no progress and realized the only damage being done was to your head, to continue to beat your head against that wall. In my short history, that refusal to quit had done more harm than good many times. The trick was to evaluate your situation and your methods, then make an informed, intelligent decision whether it made more sense to continue than to stop, or maybe even to reroute. And when you were lying on the floor of a forest, and you were cold, thirsty, and hungry, and when your only way out appeared to be moving forward even if it looked like there were obstacles but you thought they might be overcome, then that was when you decided not to quit.

So, what was my current obstacle? Well, it wasn't a brick wall; it was merely a chain link fence. And, as I had seen when shining my light on it, it wasn't a particularly good chain link fence, sagging toward me. Still, it presented more of an obstacle than the fallen tree had. It was taller and I didn't have the option of crawling around it. Nevertheless, it wasn't an insurmountable obstacle. I knew I had to find a way to get to the other side, though even that held no real promise of absolute safety. My guess was that the panther, using the tree as a take-off spot—and maybe even from ground level—could easily clear the fence, so I wasn't really safe regardless of which side I was on. On the other hand, maybe it would be enough of a deterrent that the cat would decide to find an easier meal. The harder I could make it for him to get to me, the better my chances. It was sorta like locking the doors and windows on your house. That wouldn't stop a determined burglar, but it might encourage that burglar to find a different, easier house to break into.

Besides, that ol' cat likely hadn't gone through basic training in summertime central Texas and "quit" just might well have been in its limited animal vocabulary.

I shined the flashlight on the fence again, looking for places where the chain link might have broken away from the top railing or from one of the line posts, the steel tubes driven into the ground at periodic intervals to which the mesh was attached. Surely there was some place where I might be able to finagle the chain link down far enough that I could worm my way through without having to climb over the top and deal with the barbed wire.

But, as I ran the flashlight's beam along the fence, nothing looked promising. Sure, it leaned my way, but the wire mesh appeared properly tied to all the posts within the reach of the light.

So maybe I could grab the top and pull it down farther, maybe even all the way to the ground, then I could slither over. I set the flashlight down and turned onto my side, then reached one hand up and gripped the top of the fence. Pulling down, as if doing a one-handed pull-up, I was able to bring it closer to the ground, but not far enough. The line posts were sturdy enough, and had been driven deep enough, to prevent success. They would lean but not flatten to the ground.

I grabbed the light again and used its beam to seek out another route. As I shone the light along the fencing, it flashed across booted feet on the other side. I guess Gabe just couldn't stay away, and he had come back to torture me some more. This time from the side of the fence I had set as my goal.

I raised the beam and shone it into his face, as he leaned with his elbows on the fence and looked down at me. He didn't even raise a hand to shade his eyes from the light. I guess that was an advantage to already being dead.

Behind me, on the other side of the tree I had scampered over, I could hear rustling in the underbrush. Soft guttural intonations told me the cat was still there, but maybe it had gotten distracted. It sounded just as far away as before I crawled over the tree.

"Are you here to help this time, or are you here just to torment me?" I asked.

"Why can't I do both?"

"I suppose you can but, as a personal favor, I'm asking you to do the former and forego the latter."

The cat screamed. The sound ran chills down my spine. At least as far down my spine as I had sensation.

"Loud, isn't he?" Gabe asked. "Better start making a little noise of your own."

"Why would I do that? Didn't we already go through this once before when you didn't like me banging a branch against the side of the plane? Why let him know where I am?"

Gabe snorted. "Oh, he already knows where you are. He probably did back by the plane, too."

"You think he sees me? Can they see in the dark?"

"Doesn't matter what he can see. He can smell you. So, if you make some noise, he'll at least know you're still alive, and that might mean a fight he doesn't want. But if he ever gets the notion that you're already dead . . . well, you get my drift."

I grabbed a length of wood lying next to me, a fallen branch. I raised up on one elbow and swung it in an arc, a hook shot, and tossed it into the brush farther down the fence line.

"This is no time for games," Gabe said. "I doubt if he plays fetch."

I grabbed a fist-sized rock and threw it in the same direction I had thrown the branch. "Maybe he'll follow the sound."

"You keep missing the point, preacher man. He's following your scent."

"Help me pull out part of that chain link so I can get to the other side."

Gabe shook his head. "I don't work that way."

"You're really not much help, are you?"

"It's not my fault." He reached for a section of fence where a tie wire affixed the mesh to a line post, but his hands simply passed through from one side to the other. "See, no grip."

"But somehow you were able to take off your jacket and give it to me. And you held the map when I was looking at it back by the plane. How did you do that if you can't physically touch things?"

"I don't really know for sure. Things are still a little fuzzy over here on the other side—and I mean that figuratively, not just on this side of the fence. I've crossed over the River Jordan, and I'm not entirely sure what the rules of the game are for me over here. Besides, if I'm a hallucination, well, I'm your hallucination, so wouldn't that mean you create the rules? And then again, maybe I really am an angel."

"I've given that one a lot of thought, and I've decided I'm not buying it. First you fly us into the ground, and now you can't do anything to help me get out of the mess you created. If you're an angel, you're the worst one I ever heard of. If I were you, I wouldn't hold my breath waiting to hear a bell ring so you can get your wings."

He straightened and crossed his arms. Puffed out his cheeks. "Now you've hurt my feelings. I'm offended."

"No, I haven't. And no, you're not. For some reason I can't quite figure out, I think you're actually pleased with yourself every time you gig me."

"Yeah, you're right. I'm not really offended."

"It's like this is all a game for you," I said.

"But you've got to be dead to play it, and that's not much fun. So, believe me, I'd rather be down there crawling in the leaves with you, with at least a chance of seeing my own wife and kids again, than to be standing over here."

He had a point. As irritating as he was, and as miserable as I was, I was still better off. I needed to remember that the next time he got on my nerves.

Which didn't take long.

"Riddle me this, preacher man," he said.

"If I never hear 'riddle me this' again, it'll be too soon."

"I hate to point this out, but there's a better than even chance I'm the last person you'll ever hear say it."

"As you like to say, point taken. Besides, I suppose you'll tell me it's just your feeble attempt at engaging in the Socratic method. You know that you're forcing me to face up to some greater truth about myself by asking all these questions."

"I hadn't thought about it that way, but I suppose you're right. Maybe I should have been a law professor. But getting back to my question before I was so rudely interrupted. You and I have been doing a lot of talking, backtracking all your decisions leading up to here. So, have you reached any conclusions? Do you think maybe it's just your time to go?"

"Let me turn that back on you. Was it your time to go?"

"I suppose it must have been, because I sure went."

"Under that theory, it's not my time because I'm still here. So, do you think it's my time or not?"

Gabe thought about that for a moment. His brow furrowed and, at length, he shook his head. "It's really not my question to answer, but I don't think so. Buying into that would be the easy way out."

"Easy way? How do you figure that?"

"Well, if you really believe that it's your time, and that God brought you here to take you, then all you'd have to do is quit. I know you think that goes against your grain, quitting and all, but wouldn't that actually be submitting to God's will? And if it's submitting to God's will, it's not really quitting, is it? So, yeah, it would be the easy way out."

"Have you not been paying attention? You're the one who died easy. You crashed the plane then got out and died. If I'm dying, I'm dying hard. I'm paralyzed. I'm cold, I'm hungry, I'm thirsty, I'm hurting, I'm scared. I've got a panther on my trail ready to tear me limb from limb. There's nothing about this that's easy."

"I don't know. It seems to me that it's living that's hard. I keep going back to you saying you don't like to quit—basic training and all that jazz—but maybe it's time. After all, maybe God has already quit on you."

"He hasn't quit."

Gabe held out his arms, palms up, in a "just look around you" gesture. "Then where is He?"

I was back to thinking maybe Gabe wasn't an angel, after all. Or if he was, he was even worse than I thought at first. Would an angel try to get me to question God? Or maybe Gabe was just forcing me to face up to some harsh realities. But I knew that he was wrong about this one.

I spoke in a soft voice. "He's here."

I meant it. For all the trauma of my circumstances, I believed it. For the first time, I was seriously considering the possibility, not just as an intellectual exercise, that he was, in fact, there for the express purpose of taking me home.

Suddenly, the panther screamed again. It sounded much closer this time. Maybe even as close as being just on the other side of the fallen tree, which was less than ten yards away. I couldn't tell for sure.

"I suppose you couldn't miss hearing that," Gabe said. "He wasn't fooled by you throwing that stuff. He's really close now, and it sounds like he's zeroing in on you."

"I know."

"Well, if God's here, I'd start thinking about becoming an atheist."

As if denying God was all that I needed to do to get rid of

that panther. But I knew better.

"That cat'll still be there whether I believe in God or not. The difference is that believing's enough to get me through whatever happens next."

Gabe smiled, as if expecting that response. "You really mean that, don't you?"

"I do. God never promised me I'd never suffer, just that he'd be there with me all the way through it."

The panther screamed again.

"Here's your chance to prove it." Gabe clapped his hands. "He's coming for you, preacher. Better start moving."

I grabbed the backpack and, with my now comfortable hook shot, flipped it over the fence. Then I rolled onto my stomach, facing the fence. If that cat attacked, it would end up on my back, a thought I tried to push from my mind.

I reached up and grabbed the chain link with both hands, like I had gripped the trunk of the fallen tree. I began pulling upward. It was actually easier than climbing over the tree because I was able to get a good grip on the chain link with my fingers. As I pulled myself upward, I released the link with one hand and reached higher, then repeated the process with the other, an upward hand-over-hand motion. It gave me a new appreciation for salmon swimming upstream.

The process seemed to take forever, but finally I found myself almost in a standing position, although neither of my legs supported any of my weight. Behind me, I heard sounds of the cat getting closer. I was sure it was just on the other side of the tree now.

I lifted the barbed wire that topped the fence with one hand and stuck my head and shoulders through the gap, across the fence beneath the barbs. I let Gabe's flight jacket protect my back as I began to wriggle my upper body over the top, until I was dangling upside down like I had been when I cleared the fallen tree.

At last, I dropped to the other side of the fence, face up on the ground.

The panther screamed. Surely, he was preparing to scale the tree now. Maybe even to use it as a springboard as I had envisioned it just a short while ago.

I rolled onto my stomach and rested my head on my arms. My shoulders ached and my head pounded. I felt a trickle of blood on the back of my neck, testimony to the rusty barbed wire as I threaded my head beneath it. I figured if I ever made it out of there, I'd need a tetanus shot. My stomach roiled, and I felt like I was about to throw up, even though I knew there was nothing in it. It had been too long since I had last eaten.

Gabe sat on the ground right next to me and leaned his back against the fence. I rolled over onto my back then, using my elbows, inched my way up to a rough sitting position next to him, with my upper back resting against the mesh.

"Well, preacher man, you really showed me something," he said. "I didn't think you could do it. Of course, I didn't think you'd get over that tree back there, either."

"Just goes to show you can't underestimate me."

He nodded. "I'll give you that."

"Besides, adrenaline's a powerful tool."

"And I wouldn't discount the hand of God, either."

I looked at him and smiled. "Just a few minutes ago, you were trying to make me doubt His existence."

He shook his head. "I wasn't trying to make you doubt. I just wanted to make sure you knew where to place your faith. And it looks like you meant all that stuff you said before about never quitting."

"You know much Old Testament?" I asked.

I considered myself somewhat of an Old Testament scholar, with a particular interest in the book of Joshua. If I lived through this and got home safely, someday I planned to write a commentary on the book, maybe another one on the book of

Isaiah. That was one of the things that shaped my belief, or at least you might call it my hope, that this wasn't the end for me. And if I didn't make it, maybe soon enough I could sit down with both Joshua and Isaiah in Heaven and have a conversation, real theological and philosophical discussions about what each of them meant when they wrote their books.

"More than you might expect," Gabe said, "but I've always been partial to the New Testament, so why don't you enlighten me?"

"'If you've run with the footmen and they wearied you, how will you contend with horses; and if in the land where you live in peace, they wearied you –'"

"'—how will you contend in the swelling of Jordan?' Yeah, I know that one. It's one of my favorite verses."

"You know what that means?" I asked.

"Sure. It's Bible-ese for 'you just think you've got it tough now; suck it up and keep on going because there's no guarantee it's going to get any better.'"

"That's rough paraphrase." I laughed. "Very rough, in fact, but I think your layman's interpretation just about nailed it. Who's to say that this—" I gestured around me at the darkness and the trees, "—instead of being my belly of Jonah's whale is nothing more than my swelling of Jordan. When I write about it, I'll just call it the 'denseness of the thicket.' And I haven't even gotten to the horses, yet. If I throw in the towel now, what would that say about me and my fair weather faith? I'd be saying let's not worry about the horses because the footmen are already too much for me. And don't get me started on the swelling of Jordan. But if God wants to take me, right here, right now, then let him take me. I'm ready."

"You just saying that, or do you really mean it?"

My head started to swim. I looked at Gabe, but he was just a blur. On the other side of the fence, I could still hear the rustling of the big cat, but now it seemed to be moving away, the sounds growing fainter. Retreating.

"Take a break, preacher man," Gabe said. "You've earned it."

Then I blacked out.

CHAPTER TWENTY-TWO

A soft light filtered through the trees to the floor of the Thicket. It fell on my face. I felt it first as a faint thermal whisper on my cheeks. Though my eyes were closed, the darkness of the night seemed to have lifted. I blinked and opened my eyes.

Daylight.

I wasn't sure how long I had been out, but I had survived a second night. I was still alive and kicking. Well, not kicking exactly, but still alive.

The last thing I remembered from the night before was fleeing a panther by climbing over a chain link fence, goaded on by Gabe. But when I looked around at my surroundings, there was no fence to be seen. The way I remembered it, I should have been leaning against it, but instead I was lying flat on my back. Where the fence should have been was nothing but flat ground, covered by a blanket of crisp leaves. A fallen tree stretched just a few feet behind me.

I remembered climbing over that tree, wriggling, actually. I had a distinct recollection of it, but I also remembered that, once I had scaled it, I found my path barred by a chain link fence. I remembered it as clear as day, which didn't mean much in the Big Thicket since day was dreary and dark. But I remembered a sagging chain link fence topped by barbed wire. I remembered climbing over it in a hand-over-hand swimming maneuver. I even remembered thinking about salmon. And I remembered scraping the back of my neck on the barbed wire and drawing blood. I reached behind me and felt my skin, searching for the start of a scratch. But all I felt was the smooth surface of my neck.

Had it been just another hallucination? I remembered Gabe leaning on the fence and harassing me. And sitting on the other side, leaning against it alongside me. Was the fence just an expanded version of the Gabe hallucination? Or maybe I had gotten those things reversed in my fragile mind. Had I scaled a fence first, followed by a tree? So, did that mean there really was a fence but it was simply on the other side of the tree and out of my line of sight? Was it topped by barbed wire or not? I supposed it didn't really matter. My memory of the fence was that it was in disrepair and rusty, obviously not maintained, so that meant there was no regular foot traffic by anyone nearby trying to maintain it. Still, my curiosity got the better of me. More importantly, I needed to know just how fragile my mind really was. I worked my way back to the tree on my elbows using my patented crawl. Then, reaching up to the fallen trunk and using my hands, I pulled myself up. Not all the way over, like I had the night before—or at least so it seemed—but just sufficiently to prop myself high enough so that I could see the other side.

No fence.

So I really must have simply imagined it. And if I had imagined a fence, had I also imagined a panther following me? Granted, I had never seen it, but I had heard it. Or had I? Had it, too, simply been another hallucination? As much as I wanted to believe I was in full control of my faculties, there was a measure of comfort in knowing that I was not in imminent danger of being slaughtered by a wild animal.

I was just about ready to lower myself back to the ground when I heard sounds in the distance. But not a panther's scream, nor even its guttural purr. Not even the rustling of leaves as it prowled about in search of prey.

It was a buzzing sound, kind of a roar. A sound I had heard before. I couldn't tell you when I had last heard it, but I knew the distinctive sound of a chainsaw. I had used them myself, cutting up tree trunks into firewood in the winter snow back in Japan, on the island of Hokkaido.

Above the sound of the whirring of the saw, a dog barked. It wasn't a loud or aggressive bark that signaled an alert or was precursor to an attack. Instead, it was more of a greeting. The kind you would expect to be accompanied by the wagging of a tail.

Then I heard sounds of children laughing. And that didn't make sense. In the middle of the Big Thicket?

I looked at my watch. Almost nine o'clock, and today was a school day. Thursday. Yet children were laughing close by. Was there a school out there? Could it be that I wasn't as deep into the woods as I thought? I knew I hadn't gotten all that far from the plane, not much more than a couple hundred yards, but could it be I was simply on the edges of the thicket, this close to people? And if so, did that mean that we were heard when we crashed Tuesday night? Had I effectively marooned myself by leaving the site of the wreckage?

All of those thoughts collided in my head, but I was incapable of drawing any conclusions, relying solely upon speculation, so long as I couldn't see.

I worked myself a little higher onto the tree trunk. I needed to see more than just what lay on the immediate other side; I needed to be able to see at least some distance. I rested my chest on top, sounds of the rough bark scraping against the leather of Gabe's flight jacket. I pushed up on my elbows to raise my head higher and broaden my field of vision.

I didn't see a school, but I still beheld a sight that filled my heart with joy. Immediately in front of me was a length of thicket, a thick stand of trees that stretched for maybe fifty yards or so, but beyond that was a clearing. Beyond the fringes of the trees, in the clearing, I saw a field or pasture of some sort. Though it was mid-January, in the dead of winter, the grass in the field was bright green, most likely some sort of winter rye. There were even stalks of corn standing on one side of the field, tied together in shocks and running along the perimeter. No ears weighed down the stalks, having already been harvested in the Fall, but the shocks remained just the same.

On the right side of the field, a crude farmhouse in need of repair stood. It was unpainted and its walls were made up of gray, faded planks of wood. The roof was tattered tarpaper, pitch black in color. Sunlight glittered on the tar. A sagging porch lined the front of the house, from one side to another. It, too, was constructed of the same gray planks, and a rickety rail traversed its width. There were a couple of rocking chairs and an ancient icebox on one side of the door, while a ragged sofa with tufts of cotton protruding from tears in the fabric sat on the other. It was the stereotype of what you might expect as the residence of a tenant farmer, poor but hardworking.

A screen door hung by one hinge across a solid wooden door that led into the house, centered on the porch. The mesh of the screen was torn and had been pulled outward, offering no protection against insects in warmer weather when the solid door might be left open. The steps leading up to the porch were in disrepair. I could see that the planks bowed up on both ends, giving them the appearance of a sideways parenthesis.

But the most important thing was that the house looked lived in, a fact borne out by a small chimney that emitted dark smoke from an interior fire.

I hadn't seen the house during my travels on my belly yesterday evening and last night, which wasn't surprising for three reasons. One was because I was too close to the ground, with only a worm's eye view in front of me. The second was because it had been too dark, with afternoon shadows cloaking everything in near blackness, followed by absolute blackness after the sun had set.

And the third had to do with trying to outpace the panther on my track—even if only in my imagination—which had kept my attention singularly focused ahead. The night before, I altered my path at one point to confront the fallen tree and then the fence. Or the tree and no fence, whichever it might have been. If I had simply turned in the opposite direction at that intersection,

I would have crawled away from the fallen tree, past the edge of the thickest of the trees, and would have spilled into the pasture. Of course, the reason why I hadn't done that last night was because the panther was on my trail, and I didn't have the luxury of time to make quick decisions. But now, the panther, real or imagined, was nowhere to be heard or seen. God was here with me, after all. I wished Gabe were there so I could rub his face in it.

My salvation was in sight. If I could just get there.

I heard sounds again. The chainsaw had ceased, but I could still make out the dog barking. And voices. High-pitched voices. The children I had heard before. Still laughing. I wished I could join in. Not with the children I heard, but with my own children. We had moved to the Dallas area just a few months earlier, but already the two older kids, Darlyne and Corky Bo, had become Dallas Cowboys football fans. Not a particularly good season this past year, five wins, eight losses, and one tie, but we still had a good time popping popcorn and watching the games on Sunday afternoons. Even Stevie enjoyed those afternoons, though he mostly just made a mess of the popcorn and played with his toys while we watched the games. And it gave Juanita a few blissful hours to herself, to read or do other things besides picking up after the kids.

It seemed as if the Cowboys had a bright future for the next few years, though. Two players made All-Pro—defensive tackle Bob Lilly and wide receiver Frank Clarke—and even one rookie player, Mel Renfro, made the Pro Bowl. There were also two "future draft" picks in the 1964 player draft that might bring some stars into the mix in a few years, like Olympic gold medal winner Bob Hayes from Florida A&M and Heisman Trophy winner from Navy, Roger Staubach. I just hoped I would be there to share those future successes with my kids.

I pulled myself up as far as I could to look over the tree. I still couldn't see a school, not even beyond the farmhouse, but sure enough, there were four children, two boys and two girls. I couldn't tell their ages, but it looked like maybe four or five years old, which explained why they weren't in school. All wore tattered overalls and, despite the cold temperatures, no coats. Of course, kids playing outside always seemed to heat up and shun coats and jackets, unlike me, who desperately longed for more warmth than Gabe's jacket provided.

But cold or not, they seemed happy as they joined hands and ran in a circle, ring-around-the-rosie style. Apparently, that was exactly what they were playing because, almost as if one, they suddenly all fell down, collapsing in fits of giggles. Then back to their feet again and around and around again, laughing almost hysterically, hands held, heads thrown back. They might not have been laughing had they known the origin of the game, that I, too, had played as a child in Fort Worth, dancing in a circle to the rhyme: *Ring around the rosie, pockets full of posies; ashes, ashes, we all fall down.*

According to folklore, the rhyme grew out of the Black Death plague of the Middle Ages, and the great London Plague of 1665, as well as other lesser plagues—if there was such a thing as a lesser plague. The Black Death was a worldwide epidemic of bubonic plague that had probably started in Asia but traveled to the shores of Europe aboard trading ships that docked in China, India, and the middle east. It then ravished the European countries, likely spread by fleas and rats, and may even have been airborne. Those same culprits were suspected of being behind the London Plague, and all told may have resulted in tens of millions of deaths.

Folklore held that "ring around the rosie" referred to the first signs of the plague, a rosie-red rash on skin. It also said that a superstition of the time called for people to stuff their pockets with flowers, notably posies, as a means to ward off the disease. To my mind, that hardly seemed like sound medical advice, but I supposed that folks in the Middle Ages were not quite so scientifically advanced. Then came that last line. "Ashes, ashes" referred to cremating those who died from the plague, and "all fall down" referred to death. Pretty grim stuff, especially for a kid's game.

I didn't know for sure that this was anything more than urban legend. I couldn't remember when I had first heard that explanation, but I had never confirmed the truth of the story. I didn't know why my mind drifted to such morbid thoughts, especially on what appeared to be the cusp of my own deliverance, but such was the curse of being a warehouse of useless information. I just hoped that I wasn't about to fall down, although I had already done so once, plummeting out of the sky. That fall had claimed my friend and pilot.

The truth of the legend didn't matter right then. If I really wanted to know the answer, I could research it once I got back to Dallas. What did matter then was how to get the attention of those children. I assumed that kids of such young ages would not be left at home alone, so surely there was at least one responsible adult nearby, either a mother inside the ramshackle house or perhaps a dad operating a chainsaw out of my field of vision. I pushed the ring-around-the-rosie story to the back of my mind, to be called back to the forefront later, if at all, from the comfort of my home.

I pulled the backpack from my shoulders and extracted my white dress shirt from it. Bracing myself as high as I could on the tree trunk, I waved the shirt over my head.

"Hey!" I yelled at the top of my lungs, which wasn't much. My throat was dry and my voice came out as a hoarse whisper. I struggled to generate some saliva, swallowed the meager amount to coat my throat, and tried again. "Hey!"

They couldn't hear me, obviously too far away. But that didn't matter. I knew now that there was life over there. Not wildlife; people. All I had to do was to crawl to them. Yes, that was all I had to do. Cover as much ground before nightfall, as had taken me a full day to cover yesterday. It was cliché, but still truthful: so close and yet so far.

But seeing the light at the end of the tunnel – provided it wasn't an oncoming train or a bear with a flashlight, or maybe a panther with a flashlight or the ghost light I had already seen – was a great motivator.

I tucked the shirt in the backpack and slipped it over my shoulders. My upper back was cramping, and I knew I didn't have enough strength left to pull myself over the tree again. The first time had worn me out, as had the climb over the apparently non-existent fence. Whether that fence was real or not, my fatigue was real.

So I began my crawl parallel along the trunk. At the end, which I estimated to be perhaps twenty to thirty feet, I would round the trunk and set on a path directly toward the field and house. And the children. I hoped they would still be there when I got close enough to be heard. I wasn't sure I had the energy or the strength to crawl all the way to the house. I desperately needed someone to come fetch me.

With each grab and pull, I listened carefully. I could still hear the children. The dog continued to bark. The chainsaw started up again. I had been heartened to hear it before, because presumably it meant an able-bodied man or woman was wielding it, one who could assist me the rest of the way to the house. The problem was that it would surely drown out my feeble efforts to yell for help. That meant I had to get closer. Much closer.

I moved with an almost rabid ferocity. Most of my strength had been drained the night before, climbing over obstacles both real and imagined, but thoughts of rescue sent streams of adrenaline coursing through my body. Rabid ferocity and speed were not the same concept, however. It must have taken me ten or fifteen minutes to reach the end of the tree, where the roots pointed haphazardly out of the ground. I rounded the corner and started heading toward . . .

But the field was no longer there. There was no green grass, there were no shocks of corn. No dilapidated farmhouse with smoke coming from the chimney. No children. No dog. No sounds of childish laughter. No ring-around-the-rosie. No barking. No buzz of a chainsaw.

Only trees. And more trees. Nothing but dark forest as far as I could see. And silence.

Could it be this was all just another hallucination? Like the chain link fence? Like Gabe? Like the panther and the ghost light and the railroad worker looking for his head? Was my imagination playing still more malignant tricks on my subconscious mind?

I felt as if the backpack weighed two hundred pounds. It seemed to drive me into the ground. I leaned on my elbows, shoulders hunched, and hung my head. Right then, quitting sounded really good.

"What's the matter?" Gabe asked.

I hadn't seen him appear, but suddenly there he was in front of me. He leaned against a tree, hands behind his back. I looked up at him but didn't answer. He stared at me for a moment, as if deciding whether to berate or ridicule me, empathize with me, or just leave me in silence.

He made his choice, a combination of berating and ridiculing.

"You're backtracking," he said. "Didn't you just shimmy over that tree yesterday? Kinda like a caterpillar, is what I saw."

"There was a house. Some kids were playing in the yard. I could hear them laughing and playing ring-around-the-rosie. And I heard someone running a chainsaw. I just turned the wrong way last night because there wasn't any sound to follow. All this is, is a little course correction." I paused, then decided to gig him like he was gigging me. "A little course correction from you might have been nice the other night."

"I think I'll ignore that rude remark."

"Telling me that means you didn't ignore it."

He waved his hand in a "what can you do" gesture. Then he looked around the tree, behind him, then back at me.

"Course correction or not, but what you described certainly would be nice if it actually existed. Except I don't see any house. And I don't see any kids. You're seeing things that just aren't there. And hearing things, too. I don't hear any laughing or chainsaws, either. It's all just a big figment of your imagination."

"You mean like you?"

"I suppose." He laughed. "Then again, you see me now, don't you? That means I'm here, unlike your kids and chainsaw operators."

"So, what do I do, Gabe?" I asked. "Huh? What now?"

"Well, you may not be seeing houses and kids, or hearing saws and laughing and ring-around-the-rosie, but I'll tell you one thing that's not a hallucination."

"Do tell."

He put his hand to the side of his head and cupped it around an ear. "Listen. Not where you're headed now, but where you were headed last night. On the other side of that tree."

"What am I listening for?"

"Figure it out for yourself. I don't want you to claim I planted the thought in your head. Just listen."

I rolled onto my back, raised my head, and cocked it like a dog. I strained to hear, hoping to again pick up the sounds of kids laughing and playing. Or chainsaws. But I didn't hear any of that.

Instead, I heard a faint humming noise. It sounded far away but grew in intensity as it drew nearer and the decibel level rose. When it was closer, I could hear it clear as a bell. It was unmistakable as it grew louder.

The roar of a truck engine. Like I had heard that first night, but much closer than that. I had been right all along. There was a highway out there somewhere. And though I might not have made much ground putting distance between myself and the plane wreckage, I had clearly closed the gap with that road.

"You hear that?" Gabe asked.

"I do." Even I heard the note of optimism in my voice.

"Sounded pretty close, didn't it?" Gabe asked.

And it did. Half a mile, maybe? A mile? I had no way of knowing how far sound carried out there. All I knew for sure was that it was closer than it had been, and that put me back on my original plan. When I left the plane to start with, I was searching for that highway. Wherever it was, and however far away it was, I had to get there.

And I had to get there soon. I wasn't sure if I could survive another night. In fact, I was pretty sure I couldn't.

So I began crawling again.

CHAPTER TWENTY-THREE

Juanita had scarcely slept the night before. It was the most scared she had been since the long hours she and Corky spent pacing at nights shortly after Stevie was born in Kyoto, Japan, in 1960 and they returned to Sapporo, when it became clear that something was terribly wrong with his health. He had been unable to keep his baby formula down, something that they initially wrote off, since both the older kids had gone through short spells like that, as well. But when this dragged on for days, it didn't take a doctor to see that this was something more than could be considered normal.

She would never forget that cold afternoon, in the midst of winter and darkness having arrived shortly before four o'clock in the afternoon, when they bundled him up and drove to a nearby hospital. There the doctor delivered what seemed to her and Corky as an indictment of their parenting: "Your baby is suffering from malnutrition."

The words stunned them both. They had obviously waited far too long to bring Stevie in for expert medical care because what this Japanese doctor was saying could easily be translated as, "Your baby is starving to death." These additional words carried with them not so much an indictment of their parenting skills, but a conviction.

After some interim treatment, they obtained permission from the Foreign Mission Board for emergency leave. With the older children in the care of another missionary family, she and Corky flew back to Texas for Stevie to be placed under the care of medical pediatric experts. Those American doctors determined that some kind of blockage in the baby's digestive tract was the culprit. As with so many frightening things, the unknown was the worst of it. Knowing what the problem was, though, usually meant a solution could be found. Such was the case then.

But such was not the case last night. Her husband was

missing and nobody knew where he was. That unknown haunted her and kept her awake all night. Pastor Gene McCombs from the First Baptist Church and his wife Mary had come over after she put the kids to bed and sat up with her into the wee hours of the night. There wasn't really anything they could do, but it still provided a measure of comfort not to be alone.

Stevie had awakened shortly after they arrived. He'd had a nightmare, he said, but he was unable to explain what it was about. She saw that he was trembling and on the verge of tears, which brought tears to her own eyes as she held her youngest and softly sang to him. She worried that he had experienced some premonition about Corky's fate, just as she feared that Corky Bo's pronouncement during supper that maybe there had been a plane crash was also a premonition. After a while, Pastor McCombs took Stevie from her and held him in his lap while he sat in a rocking chair and gently rocked him to sleep. She sat on the couch, while Mary sat beside her and held her hand.

The next morning, a deacon from the church arrived to pick up Corky Bo and Darlyne to take them out to breakfast at a local diner, then on to school. Corky's mom and her own parents were already on their way from Fort Worth. She hadn't called them the night before because she didn't want to seem alarmist, but by morning, with no word from the local authorities in southeast Texas, it was clear that she must expect the worst. So she had called.

Now, Gene and Mary sat with her again, at the breakfast table, sipping coffee and waiting silently for some word of hope. A word that seemed increasingly far away with each passing minute.

CHAPTER TWENTY-FOUR

Thursday, as the clock approached noon, Velma Withers and Irene Gooden, two elderly widowed sisters who lived together in Woodville, along the edges of the Big Thicket, prepared lunch in their kitchen. They lived in a wooden frame, one-story house with two bedrooms—though the sisters shared one, separate beds, of course—a parlor, kitchen, and one bathroom, barely 1,000 square feet in size. The house was tastefully furnished as only elderly women can do, with antique furniture that had likely been purchased new, flowers and lace doilies, and store-bought artwork hanging on the walls.

Velma and Irene had been living together ever since Velma's husband Joe, a mechanic at one of the local service stations, had passed away suddenly of a heart attack two years earlier.

Irene, older by two years, also widowed and on her own for more than a decade, had immediately offered to take Velma in since her sister had no visible means of support. Velma had never held a job and, after her husband's death, was unable to meet the monthly mortgage on the small two-bedroom house she had shared with Joe. Mortgage insurance had seemed like such an unnecessary expense when you could barely make ends meet but, after Joe's death, it had seemed so short-sighted not to have borne that expense. Velma and Joe had been childless, so it fell to the big sister to step in.

Both women were in their late 70s and had developed a rhythm to their daily lives. Morning prayers and Bible reading, like good east Texas Southern Baptists, then a light breakfast of oatmeal and dry toast, followed by housekeeping, particularly vacuuming, sweeping, and dusting, whether needed or not, then lunch and, in the afternoon, watching their "stories" on television. That was the highlight of their days, the opportunity to live vicariously through characters they had grown to know as well as if they were family.

The sisters were both hopelessly hooked on *The Edge of Night*, *The Secret Storm* and *As the World Turns*, all on CBS, their favorite channel. In fact, they almost felt like traitors any time they switched the channel to ABC to watch the relatively new show *General Hospital* or over to NBC for *Search for Tomorrow*.

Neither of the sisters had slept well the night before, or Tuesday night before that, for that matter. In fact, after turning in at their customary time on Tuesday, nine-ish, shortly after *The Red Skelton Show* on CBS ended, they had been awakened by a loud noise sometime after 10 o'clock.

"What was that?" Irene asked, bolting up in her bed.

"I don't know."

Velma pushed aside her quilt and sat on the edge of the bed. She slipped her feet into a pair of slippers and, clad in red striped flannel pajamas, got up.

"Stay there," she said. "I'll go see."

But Irene, never one to do as she was told—in fact, she resented being told what to do, especially in her own house—followed her sister into the tiny parlor. They both looked out the window but saw nothing other than darkness. A fog had settled in, obscuring their view.

"Maybe we just imagined we heard something," Irene said.

Velma sniffed. "How can two people imagine the same thing at the same time?"

"Well, then, it was probably a car crash on the highway. Sheriff's deputies will take care of it. That's none of our concern."

Irene conceded that her sister had a point, so they both returned to their beds, content to leave the noise as an unsolved mystery. But the excitement had kept either of them from going back to sleep easily, so they both seemed to be in a state of sleep-deprivation when they did their chores the next morning. It created a sluggishness that carried over to Thursday morning as well when they finished their morning chores a bit later than usual.

They had the radio tuned to a local Beaumont station that played the kind of music they so enjoyed, primarily big band music and oldies from their youth, while they prepared the noon meal.

"Will you hand me that tuna fish?" Velma asked. She opened a package of bread and set the unsliced loaf on a wooden cutting board.

She positioned her bread knife on the edge of the bread and began removing the end crust with a sawing motion. Irene opened the icebox door and took out a bowl covered with tin foil, containing the tuna salad concoction they had made the day before for sandwiches. She had just handed it to her sister when, following a commercial break on the radio, the station's news announcer interrupted the broadcast.

"Sheriff's deputies and Civil Air Patrol members continue their search for a missing single engine aircraft that disappeared after taking off from a small air strip outside of Evadale Tuesday night at approximately ten o'clock p.m. It is believed that the plane might have crashed in the Big Thicket shortly after takeoff. Residents are encouraged to call local authorities with any information. And now, back to our regularly scheduled music program."

Velma and Irene exchanged glances.

"Did he say the plane took off Tuesday night at ten?" Irene asked.

"Yes."

Irene lifted the receiver from the phone on the wall next to the icebox and dialed "O" for the operator.

"Can I help you?" a female voice answered.

"Please connect me with the Sheriff's Department."

A few seconds later, she heard another female voice. "Tyler County Sheriff's Office."

"This is Irene Gooden. My sister and I live in Woodville, right next to the Thicket, and we just heard a report on the radio about a missing airplane."

"Yes, ma'am. Do you have any information about that?"

"I think so. Tuesday night, we went to bed at our usual time, around nine or so, but probably a little after ten o'clock, we heard a loud crashing noise that woke us up. We thought it was a car accident on the highway, but we know better now. It just had to be that airplane."

CHAPTER TWENTY-FIVE

I felt my strength seeping away. Each stroke forward with my hands dug in shallower in the dirt and when I pulled with my elbows, the distance I covered seemed to lessen with each stroke. I had already recalibrated my initial calculations of how long it would take me to get out of the woods, and now it appeared as if even the revised numbers needed serious recalibration. The traffic sounds I heard earlier came intermittently, at best, and they seemed no closer now than they had when Gabe first directed my attention to them. I was starting to believe I was on a fool's errand and that maybe it was time to quit. Yes, quit.

My body made that decision for me when, at last, I simply couldn't go any farther. I had no strength to reach forward, no reserves to pull myself along. I rolled onto my back and closed my eyes. I felt as if the very life was oozing out of my body the same way my strength oozed from my fingertips.

"Are you quitting?" Gabe asked. He had done another of his disappearing acts but reappeared again, and he was now apparently a mind reader.

"Just resting." He and I both knew better, but I still couldn't bring myself to say the word or even acknowledge it.

"If you say so," he said.

I opened my eyes and looked up at him. "How far have I gone?" I asked.

"As the crow flies or as the worm crawls?"

"Just answer me."

He looked back in the direction from which I had started and shook his head. "I hate to tell you this, but I can still see the plane."

I raised up on an elbow and followed the direction of his gaze. All I saw was shadows and trees.

"I guess your eyesight gets better after you die," I said.

"I guess so. Or maybe it's some kind of X-ray vision like Superman's. My best estimate, you've covered about two hundred fifty, maybe three hundred yards. I guess that's a good news/bad news thing."

"How do you figure?"

"Well the bad news is that you're still pretty close to the plane. The good news is that, since you were so worried at the start about getting too far away from the plane, you're still pretty close to it. In case a search team finds the plane."

I closed my eyes again and lay back down.

"What are you thinking?" Gabe asked.

"About Juanita and the kids. They must be sick with worry by now. If we'd left when we originally planned, we should have been home almost twenty-four hours ago."

"That's probably about right. So some more good news is that there have to be search parties out looking for us right now. Might even have started last night."

"There's an awful lot of ground to cover." I remembered other calculations I had made in my mind before I started crawling about the sheer vastness of the acreage that would have to be searched.

"Maybe I should see what I can do about steering them in your direction," Gabe said.

I popped up on an elbow again. "Can you do that?"

"I don't know. Maybe. Assuming they're out there. Like I said before, I haven't quite figured out the rules, yet. But there's no harm in trying, is there?"

"Of course not."

"Okay, tell you what. You wait here and let me see what I can do."

"Where else would I go?"

But he had already disappeared.

I lay flat on my back and closed my eyes. I even had the sensation of feeling relief, though I couldn't tell if it was because

I had confidence he could do what he said, or if it was just gratitude that he had left me alone with my thoughts. Or maybe it was that I was starting to accept the inevitable. It would sure eliminate some of the stress of worrying about getting out if I simply made peace with the fact that I never would.

I shook that thought off as too negative. As bad as my situation was, as long as I was alive, as long as I drew breath, there was still some hope, no matter how scant it might be.

As I lay there, I had the impression of floating on my back on the surface of dark water. Periodically, my body dipped below the surface, the water blotting out any vision, then I popped back above the surface, gasping and sputtering for breath. But each time I came back up, I felt weaker. Not the kind of fatigue caused by the effort to crawl but a complete emptying of energy and strength from my body. I couldn't understand what was going on. That was the first time I had experienced something like that since the crash.

On one of the occasions that I re-surfaced, I opened my eyes and looked around. Looking for Gabe, to see if he had succeeded in steering searchers my way. It seemed as if he had been gone a long time, but I couldn't be sure. I checked my watch. Not even noon yet, but then again, I didn't know what time it was when I last saw him. He had always seemed to be there when I needed him to keep me talking, to goad me into action, to keep my mind functioning. That all gave me a certain measure of hope. But I needed him now, and he was nowhere to be seen. It was as if I was, finally, truly on my own.

"You're dying," I said to myself. I might have even said it out loud, I didn't know, but I distinctly remembered formulating that frightening thought in my tortured mind. It was followed almost immediately by the clichéd, "But you're too young to die." Funny how tragedy can bring out all of life's little clichés. But of course there is often truth in clichés. That was probably how they came to be clichés in the first place.

But cliché or not, it was a very real thought. I was thirty-seven years old, only out of school for less than ten years. Oh, sure, I had been involved in pastoring churches and mission work, but I was still essentially a student during much of that time. I had a wife and three young children who were counting on me to come home. Counting on me to make sure they had a roof over their head and food on the table – another cliché, perhaps? But I truly was too young to die, wasn't I? According to all the charts and tables I had seen, I hadn't even lived half my life.

I went back over in my mind the things I had discussed with Gabe and my own inner thoughts that had visited me since Tuesday night. I again reconsidered the decisions I had made that led me to that tiny air strip in Evadale, Texas, in January of 1965. Even if the decision to leave the mission field and to join the Evangelism Division in Texas had been part of God's will for my life, maybe it was decisions I had made after arriving in Texas that diverged from that will. Like maybe the particular trip that brought me to my current state.

But I quickly dismissed the thought. On the day of our arrival in southeast Texas, I had the opportunity to share the gospel with a man in the community at whose home Gabe and I had stopped, after landing at the air strip, to use the phone to call the church to be picked up. The man was an admitted alcoholic, who told us, "You know, today is my day off, and I started to go into town, but I knew if I did, I'd just get drunk. The truth is, for some reason I can't explain, I've just been kind of waiting around here is if I was waiting for somebody to come."

Before we left his house, the man prayed and God answered his prayer for salvation. When I reconstructed the memory of that day, I concluded that if I'd ever made a trip in my life that the Lord was in, it was that trip.

I finally came to the conclusion that every decision I had made, from going to seminary and to Japan, then back to Texas to the Evangelism Division, and right up to and including the trip to Evadale, had been following God's will for my life. I *knew* I was following him. So, wasn't that really good news? Wasn't it great to be able to say I was solidly in God's will?

Well, not necessarily. Not if you were lying paralyzed on the floor of the Big Thicket and were looking for a way out. Because if I had made wrong or selfish decisions along the way and had strayed from God's will, I always had the option of saying something like, "Well, Lord, I rebelled, like Jonah. I shouldn't have come to the Evangelism Division, but I should have gone back to Japan. Now, if you'll just get me out of this mess, I'll straighten up and fly right. I'll repent in sackcloth and ashes." Like the mouse who said, "Forget the cheese, just let me out of this trap."

But I couldn't say that. And it begged the question of whether my rebellion went back farther than that? Maybe I was being too short-sighted in reviewing and judging my actions over my adult years. Had I perhaps committed some unpardonable sin as a youth, engaged in some unforgiveable rebellion, that had simply festered until the punishment could be meted out decades later?

That question set my mind back to a much earlier period in my life, to a time when I did, in fact, go through a period of real rebellion. Back to my junior high and, more significantly, my high school years.

Because I was double-promoted in grammar school, I found myself at a disadvantage at trying to play sports, particularly football, in junior high and high school because I was younger and smaller than those at my grade level. There was also an earlier time when I suffered from a glandular disturbance that kept me from participating in sports as much as I would have liked, anyway, so I was not only too young and too small by the time I reached junior high, but I was also too inexperienced.

As a result, I became more withdrawn, spending most of my time outside of school alone. I developed a particular interest in reading books, mostly adventure books and even encyclopedias, but that was just a way of keeping to myself and building fantasy worlds.

When I started junior high school, my interest in athletics was rekindled by the heightened emphasis on sports one finds at that higher level of school, something that carried on into high school. In my last year of junior high, despite my youth and size, I played on the school football team and achieved some level of success.

Besides the satisfaction that came with that type of success, another benefit was being accepted as part of the "in" group at school, as athletes so often were, whether deserved or not. When you were part of that "in" crowd, though, you never really thought about whether your place was merited.

But that feeling of acceptance deepened a desire to continue to be accepted. Once you were in, you would do almost anything to stay in. I was so impressionable and eager to be one of the gang, that I closed my eyes to the fact that the crowd I ran with wasn't necessarily interested in wholesome endeavors. I made good grades and was even elected class vice-president my last year of junior high, but I found myself more and more drawn to decidedly unchristian activities.

When I reached high school, it was a different matter, altogether. I still wanted to be part of the in group but starting on the low end of the social totem pole at Polytechnic High wreaked havoc with my already shaky self-confidence. For one thing, the double promotion in my early school years really left me on the outside, as far as football was concerned. Because I was younger, only thirteen-years-old when I started at Poly, the gap in size between a youngster like me and junior and senior football players was far more significant than what I faced before. Despite my modicum of success on the gridiron in junior high, because I was so much smaller than those who thrived on the high school football team, I decided not to go out for football that first year.

In order to maintain my social status, at least among my class with whom I had graduated from junior high, and to strive for social status with my new classmates in high school, I found myself even more engaged in questionable activities while trying to stay in their good graces. Many of them weren't Christians, nor were many of their activities something that my parents would have tolerated had they known of them. I even found myself with less time for activities such as Sunday school and church, often ditching one or both of those activities, much to my parents', particularly my mother's, dismay.

Among other things, I discovered girls, alcohol, and tobacco, a high school boy's personal triumvirate of vice opportunities in the early 1940s. I thought I was getting away with much of my questionable activities, thinking I was concealing them from my parents. I was even bold enough to bring a pipe into the house, which I smoked outside so as not to leave telltale odors in the house. I didn't know why I thought that was a good idea nor why it would go undetected, but it would come back to haunt me.

I kept my pipe buried beneath some clothes in a bureau drawer, but one day I found it gone and a handwritten letter in its place. I remember that my hands were shaking as I unfolded the page and began reading what was written in my mother's handwriting.

Dear Corky:

I sure do hate it so bad that I smelled so bad that I was found by your mother. I could hear her sniff sniffing around and next thing I knew she was going through the drawer cleaning everything. I dashed from one end of the drawer to the other trying my best to keep hid but she took every garment out and all I could do was to just hang my head in shame. I felt so little and cheap when I looked up into your mother's face and saw that disappointed expression. I knew all the time I didn't belong here, some thug should have owned me. I tried every way to keep out of your sight to begin with for I knew a nice boy like you shouldn't own a nasty little old scamp like me. I am to be pitied; there really is no place for a thing like me so will you please bury me beneath the sod that I may rest throughout eternity in peace.

Yours truly with regret,
Your little old nasty pipe

Mom never said anything else to me about the pipe, but I learned my lesson—though likely not the one she hoped I would learn. The lesson she surely hoped for was that I would quit the nasty habit. The lesson I learned was to keep all of my nasty habits far removed from the house so as to avoid detection. She couldn't find what wasn't there, my thinking went.

I tried out for football my junior year, starting with spring training during the latter semester of my sophomore year. I had grown a little so, although I was still comparatively small, I had made up some ground on my contemporaries. Then I developed a bad sinus infection just prior to the start of school the next Fall. Although it didn't cause me to miss any of the season, it did affect my strength and stamina during the first part of the season, so I had very little playing time in games. I failed to letter, which was a devastating blow to my ego, as it likely would have been to any high school athlete. Unfortunately, I wasn't mature enough to realize that those were just the breaks, but instead I found myself blaming God for what I perceived as his failure, not mine.

This was in 1943 and World War II was in full swing. I was just as influenced by the restlessness that affected so many of my classmates, as well as the youth, in general, across the country. I had not yet turned sixteen – and wouldn't until the summer between my junior and senior years—but I longed to join the military and be a part of something that was larger than myself.

I became increasingly rebellious at home. Both of my brothers were married and out of the house, and had been for some time, which left me as the only child still home. I resented the discipline of my parents, particularly that of my father, and chose to assert my independence by refusing to go to church completely. In fact, I spent very little time at home, spending most of my time with my friends, hanging out in pool rooms and night clubs, even though I was underage. I began developing a movie-style tough-guy persona. Looking back on it, I realized that I had become the very type of boy my mother didn't want me to run around with.

By my senior year, I had gotten even worse. One of the aggravating factors was that I was healthy and able to play football again at the level I expected of myself. I was actually pretty good at it, even earning honorable mention honors on the all-district team. I became awfully impressed with my own success and, again looking back, I saw that I became unbearably vain and cocky, as so many high school athletes are wont to do, with an unjustified sense of entitlement. And alongside that air of invincibility that so often accompanied youth, came deeper and deeper rebellion against God, with the conviction that I could do as I pleased without consequence. Master of my own fate and all that.

But through it all, I also found myself developing a growing restlessness and unhappiness. The harder I tried to have a good time, the more dissatisfied I became. I chalked it up to that same sense of restlessness gripping America's youth in a time of war, but looking back on it later, I realized that it was God convicting me.

I thought the football scholarship to SMU would be the answer. After all, my parents had refused to grant their permission for me to join the Marines, and so being on a new athletic team once again gave me a sense of place that I hadn't felt since the end of my senior season at Poly. I was sure I could duplicate my gridiron success at SMU and then, who knew, maybe a professional career. Of course, I didn't really consider the latter much of a possibility, given my still relatively small size for a football player, but not all dreams were realistic dreams. Sometimes it's the lack of realistic possibility that qualifies it as a dream to start with.

Then came the ankle injury that ended my playing career before it really even got started. I was leading a dive play into the line during a scrimmage, blocking for our fullback. I made contact with the opposing linebacker and tried to turn him one way so the fullback could cut the other. Unfortunately, when that fullback planted his foot to cut, he planted it squarely on my ankle. Career over.

I decided that, if I couldn't play football, then I really didn't want to be at SMU. After all, without the scholarship, I never would have gone there in the first place. When I sought permission from my parents to drop out, that led me to the bargain I made with my mother: If I would agree to start going to church again, she would permit me to drop out of school.

That was the best bargain I ever struck, because it led in almost a straight line to Juanita. But it also led to something else.

CHAPTER TWENTY-SIX

My church membership while in high school at Poly was at Sagamore Hill Baptist Church, but by the time I left SMU, Mom was attending nearby Polytechnic Baptist Church, where she also taught Sunday School. Our membership remained back at Sagamore Hill, though.

True to my agreement to return to church again if allowed to drop out of SMU, I began attending Poly Baptist with Mom. It was hard to recall specifically whose idea it was for me to go to Poly, but it was most likely Mom's way of keeping tabs on me. It was at Poly that I got involved in the music program with Dallas Alford, which also first brought Juanita to my attention. But more than that, it was my involvement there that led me to become more and more convicted of my rebellion against God. I began to actually see, with my own eyes, the differences between the lives of those living within God's will and my own, living without. I had been trying so hard to have a good time in worldly pleasures, but for some strange reason, my friends at the church seemed to be getting much more out of life than I was. And that really rankled me.

Then came New Year's Eve of 1944. Poly Baptist held a watch night service to ring out the old year, and I attended with Mom. I'd been going there for a couple of months with her, and she decided, with my concurrence, that it was time for both of us to move our membership from Sagamore Hill to Poly, which we did at the service. But old habits die hard. As soon as the service was over, I headed into town to meet some of my friends for an old-fashioned New Year's Eve hoopla, and to participate in whatever stereotypical debauchery might come with it.

I knew my friends were *somewhere* in Fort Worth that evening, but I had failed to pin down a specific location beforehand. That might not have mattered, anyway, because our typical procedure was to bounce from saloon to saloon and nightclub to nightclub, kinda like a floating crap game. After I left the church, I went to practically every nightclub in town, starting with our usual haunts then branching out to others. I must have been two steps behind them because I struck out at each location. I figured I had two choices: I could keep looking for them or I could go home.

Make that three choices. No teenage boy wanted to stay home on New Year's Eve, and I sure didn't, not the social animal I had become. Although I craved the companionship of my non-church friends, that didn't appear to be in the cards. The only place where I could find people I knew was back at Poly Baptist. In typical Baptist fashion, a second service was planned for that night, after the watch service earlier that evening, to ring in the new year. Not my first choice—or even my second—but I couldn't find anyone else to hang out with. So, since I had nothing better to do and I wasn't ready to go home yet, I went back to the church for that midnight service.

When I got there, the service had already started. I slipped quietly in the back door and took a seat on the rear pew. I may have promised Mom I'd start going to church again, but I never said I wouldn't be a "back row Baptist."

The preacher for the service was just preparing to deliver his sermon as I settled in. He was a young man, not much older than I, or at least he didn't look much older, probably only in his early to mid-twenties. I didn't know him nor had I ever heard him preach before, but I had an immediate favorable impression of him as he approached the pulpit to speak. He was strikingly handsome, almost movie star handsome, with neatly-cut and combed brown hair and a million dollar smile. He was snappily dressed in a dark-colored three-piece suit. I remember wishing I had a suit like that and that, if I did, I could wear it as well as he did. Frankly, he was the first preacher I ever remembered seeing who appeared as if he could really do something besides preach—like be that movie star he looked like—if he wanted to. Yet, for some reason, he had chosen to preach.

Thinking about Dallas Alford and his leadership in the music program at Poly Baptist, and now listening to this young man who obviously had so much going for him, I began to seriously think, for the first time, that there might really be something to this whole "living for the Lord" thing, after all. I had heard about it my whole life, having grown up in the church before deciding to prioritize other things, only to now be back in a church pew on New Year's Eve. I wasn't driven by any desire to live a Christian life, but I was in church only because it was the condition I had to agree to in order to get permission to drop out of SMU. I wondered what that said about me.

After looking this young preacher over, though, and deciding he might be worth listening to, I did just that: I listened to him. And, lo and behold, as I absorbed the words he spoke, it seemed as if he were speaking directly to me. It was as if there were no one else present in the building. Just a hard-headed, rebellious teenager in the back row and a handsome, eloquent stranger behind the pulpit.

The text he used was Ezekiel 3:18. I didn't have my Bible with me, but I listened as he read the verse aloud: *When I say unto the wicked, Thou shalt surely die; and thou givest him not warning, nor speakest to warn the wicked from his wicked way, to save his life; the same wicked man shall die in his iniquity; but his blood will I require at thine hand.*

I had heard that verse before, but it hadn't really made any impact on me. Not like it did that night. As that young preacher spoke about Christian responsibility, about the duty to warn others about the consequences of sin, I thought about how I had abdicated my own responsibilities and duties. I had friends who weren't believers, and I knew it, but I had never said a word to them about my Christian faith. Given my own personal lifestyle, they might well have just laughed it off if I had ever tried. They might not even believe that I was a Christian, since there was nothing about my life to suggest that I was.

I became aware of my own personal, shameful predicament. I was running with a crowd that was going straight to hell – and I was helping them get there. Already, I knew of two friends, both non-Christians, who had been killed in an automobile accident and I had never once spoken to them about heaven. My life had sealed my lips. Would the blood of those two boys be required at my hands?

As these devastating realities soaked into my consciousness, I became at once both fearful and ashamed. What would I tell the Lord when it came time for me to enter heaven? What could I say when He asked about those boys and my silence? I turned it over in my mind, running through one flimsy excuse after another—the time wasn't right, they weren't ready to listen, I planned to do it later. But I realized that not one of those so-called reasons would excuse me. My duty was to speak, not to dictate the response. I concluded that I didn't want the blood of any of my other friends on my hands. So I decided, right there and then, to fully surrender my life to the Lord and His service.

Then came the invitation, as we Baptists called it, or altar call as I had heard it termed by other denominations—or altercation, if you combined the two. But this one was different from most I had seen. Typically, we stood and sang while the preacher exhorted people, on an individual basis, to walk down the aisles to the front. But that night, the preacher invited the entire congregation, every last one of us, to come to the altar at the front and to close out the last thirty minutes of the old year, and ring in the new, on our knees in prayer.

Now, I had prayed before, many times, but just about all, if not all, of my prior prayers had been perfunctory, sometimes almost by rote. I typically just spoke the words I had heard others use in their prayers and adopted them as my own, or I used other pet phrases I had learned in Sunday school or vacation Bible School, but without any conviction behind them.

That night, though, I walked to the front in a state of deep conviction. Unlike most invitations I had suffered through, I felt God speaking specifically to me, almost as if I were the only one there, much as it seemed the young preacher's sermon was aimed solely at me. I got down on my knees and, for the first time that I could remember, actually poured out my heart to the Lord, confessed my sins one by one, and asked for forgiveness. I felt as if there was no way God could ever forgive those things I had done and those I had failed to do. But when I humbled myself and earnestly sought His forgiveness, I found a loving Father who was ready to receive the prodigal son back home. There was no "holy laughter" involved, but it was certainly a soul-baring, soul-cleansing experience for me.

Over the next few days, I became increasingly aware that the old restlessness and vague unhappiness that had plagued my life was gone. Those feelings that had motivated my desire to find thrills and excitement in alcohol or unwholesome activities, to join the Marines in order to feel as if I were doing something meaningful or worthwhile, or that had driven me to leave SMU scarcely a few months into the school year—all of those were gone. Instead, I found that meaning for which I had been searching, to no avail, in every dive and bar and nightclub in Fort Worth, and I found it in the last place I had thought to actually look: in a church.

I soon also found that much of my thinking and planning for the future was now somehow wrapped up in the church and the Lord's work. When singing in the quartet, I found new meaning in the words to the songs that had eluded me before. More and more, I wanted people to know the happiness I found in doing God's work, and I began to entertain thoughts of how wonderful it would be to spend my life telling others about it.

Then one day I had a conversation with Dallas Alford that added a new dimension to what I was beginning to think and feel. We had finished quartet practice at the church, and the others had gone home. I stayed and helped Dallas clean up before leaving, when he asked me to join him for coffee. We went to a nearby coffee shop and settled into a booth, then placed our orders.

After the waitress brought our coffees, he asked, "Corky, what are your plans for the future?"

"Well, I want to join the military." That thought, and desire, had not completely faded. Besides, it almost seemed like a good place-holder, to buy some time while figuring out what I really wanted to do with my life. "I think I owe it to my country to do that, like a lot of my friends have," I added, "but I'm still too young to join without parental consent." I laughed and added, "And that seems like a non-starter."

He laughed, too. "I think that's fine, but I'm talking more long-term than that. Let's say you do join the marines or the army. Would you consider that as a career?"

"No, not really. I just want to do my part in the war effort." And have that place-holder.

"So, what about after that?" he asked. "Have you ever felt led to go into full-time ministry?"

If he had asked me that just a couple of months earlier, I would have laughed. But the truth was, that was exactly what I was thinking. I just didn't know what direction to go with that thought, and it occurred to me that military service might buy the time I needed to figure that out. Like I said, a place-holder.

"If I went into the ministry, what would I do?" I asked. "I'm sure not any kind of preacher." I was painfully aware of how poorly I would stack up against the young preacher from New Year's Eve.

"What about doing something with music?" he asked.

I supposed that made some sense. I was fully conscious of my limitations but, after all, I could sing a little. I supposed maybe I could give my sole talent to God. But when I thought about that, I realized how presumptuous that sounded. I didn't really feel any divine call, but I simply felt a need in my own life to do something meaningful, so the notion of giving that talent to God was more to suit myself than to answer to God's call. As if God really needed my meager talents.

I would later learn, though, that God's call can come in different ways. There's no "one size fits all," but what was important was to surrender oneself and be open to the call when it came. It wasn't that God needed my meager talents, but that I needed to entrust those talents to Him. And so, one Sunday shortly after that, during worship services, I found myself walking the aisle again, this time to publicly surrender to full-time Christian service in the field of Christian music. I never dreamed at the time that He would ever want me to preach. If He hadn't, maybe I wouldn't be lying on the ground in a forest in southeast Texas in the middle of the winter wondering how I had gotten there.

At the same time, what if it turned out that He really hadn't wanted me to preach but that He had, instead, wanted me to stay in music. Was that where I went wrong? Could that be why I had ended up where I was? After all, that switch from music to preaching precipitated mission trips to Japan while at Baylor, which led to enrollment at the seminary as a ministerial student, which led to pastorates at various churches, which led to moving to Japan as a missionary. And that last one was the springboard back to Texas and my present uncomfortable predicament.

But almost as soon as the thought crossed my mind, I banished it. There was no doubt in my heart and mind that, although God had first gotten my attention with music, all along his purpose for my life was to preach the gospel.

Besides, that was all in the past. Yes, I had rebelled against God in the foolishness of my youth, but I had repented of my rebellion and followed, as best I knew how, the Lord's will in my life, which had taken me to the mission field and on to the field of evangelistic preaching. The fact that, for the past two decades, I had been earnestly trying to live my life in the center of God's will, now left me with no real solution to my current dilemma. If you had deliberate rebellion, like I did in the past, then you could always repent, which I did.

But new rebellion, certainly new deliberate rebellion, required new repentance. And even if it was inadvertent rebellion—not deliberately disobeying God but more being selfish and disregarding God's will for your life, or maybe being negligent and simply missing God's will due to inattention – you still had the prospect of possibly getting off the hook through repentance. You just had to promise to straighten up and fly right. That was what I had done that New Year's Eve back in Fort Worth all those years ago. Since then, I had, to the best of ability and recollection, strived to stay in God's will. I hadn't made any choice without first seeking the Lord's leadership. So now, looking back, I couldn't see that I had any rebellion to renounce, no wrong decision to correct, no disobedience to be redeemed. Not even any negligence to make amends for. Nothing to pledge to get me out of the whale's belly.

So, what do you do then?

I was forced to come to the brutal thought that maybe, just maybe, the Lord had led me back to the States from Japan, then home to Texas, and even on that specific trip to Evadale, because that was the time and that was the circumstance for Him to call me home. If so, that meant I was still in God's will, even if that meant lying paralyzed in the woods on a cold winter's day. And even if that meant dying. We all have to die sometime. I simply had to accept it and make peace with it.

And so I prayed, "All right, Lord, if that's the case, then that's fine. I'm ready to go."

Then I thought about my family. What would happen to Juanita and the kids? How would they make it without a husband and father? Every little girl needs her daddy. Who would teach my boys to throw a baseball, catch a football, and cast a lure into a lake looking for a lunker bass? Who would help Juanita support the family financially? And emotionally? Just as quickly as those questions reared their head, the answers appeared, too. If the Lord was ready to take me, if that was His will, that didn't mean that He would abandon my family. No, I knew He would take very good care of them even in my absence.

But what about that sense of divine appointment or purpose I had felt? I hadn't experienced a Shantung revival in Japan, but what if it was yet to come? What if the Lord really did have something more in store for me, whether here in Texas or elsewhere? Would He take me now without allowing that to come to fruition?

So I continued my prayer and said, "Lord, if you still have something in mind for me, if you have further plans, even though it's taken a miracle to preserve me thus far, I want you to perform another one, if that destiny is still there."

Then I began to sink beneath the dark water once again. As I did, I didn't know if I was going to come up this time or not, or whether this one would be the last. To be honest, if it had been up to me to cast the deciding vote, in my pain and exhaustion, I wasn't real sure what I would have chosen.

CHAPTER TWENTY-SEVEN

By early Thursday afternoon, CAP had three small planes in the air, each with a pilot and co-pilot, above the portion of the Thicket that bounded the home of the widowed sisters. The pilots segmented the area, so as not to duplicate efforts, and began making sweeps over the trees, one side to the other before making U-turns and retracing the route one grid box over.

Another party gathered on the ground in a field behind the elderly sisters' home. There were fourteen men in all, consisting of Tyler County sheriff's deputies and Woodville police officers, as well as the pastor and one of the deacons from the Baptist Church in Kountze where Corky had been two nights before. The men, all wearing heavy coats and boots, mingled around Tyler County Sheriff Grady Ray and awaited their marching orders.

Sheriff Ray addressed the men before they began their search.

"The report we got was that the plane might have gone down not too far from here Tuesday night. That means they've been on the ground for two nights. We don't know whether they're still alive, but I'm an optimist, and I choose to believe that they are. We've been lucky that the temperatures haven't dropped below freezing, but it's been cold and they've probably been without food and water, as well, so time is of the essence. We've still got several hours of daylight, but you boys who live around here know how dark it can get underneath all those trees.

"I want you to spread out, maybe a first down apart. For you non-football fans—and I can't believe there are any of those here in east Texas—that's ten yards."

Even though it was hard to conceive of any red-blooded male in east Texas not being a rabid football fan, his attempt to lighten the mood failed. No one so much as broke a smile.

That was fine with him. It meant they were taking this

seriously.

"What kind of plane is it, Sheriff?" a Woodville cop asked.

"I understand it's a single engine Mooney Mark 21, white and green. But I don't think you really need to know that. If you come across any wrecked plane on the ground or in the trees, I'm betting it's the one we're looking for."

He looked around at each of the searchers.

"Okay, boys, let's bring these two fellas home to their families."

At that, the bunched up group of men fanned out along a perimeter outside the edge of the forest.

Then they began a straight-ahead sweep into the thickness of the trees.

CHAPTER TWENTY-EIGHT

As the darkness enveloped me, I dreamed. A lot of people put stock in dreams. I never had before, but this one was different. A strange dream, almost surreal. I found myself an observer in a large office high in a skyscraper. I had never been in that office before, nor even in that building. There was one wall that was nothing but floor-to-ceiling windows with a view toward a mountain range, with snow-capped peaks. I could almost imagine that one of those peaks was Mount Fujiyama—Mount Fuji—the highest mountain in Japan, visible on a clear day from Tokyo. Both Buddhism and Shintoism treated it reverently in their mythology. But Mount Fuji was a singular peak, unlike this one set in the midst of a range of peaks. I had never seen this range before, not even in pictures.

The room itself was typical of a businessman's office—a very successful businessman. A row of filing cabinets, made of rich mahogany wood, lined one complete wall of the office. A similar row of cabinets covered the opposite wall. Each drawer bore a letter of the alphabet. I didn't know how I knew it, but the files inside bore names of people.

On the fourth wall of the office, opposite the windows but flanked by the rows of filing cabinets, was a massive desk, made of the same mahogany, that stretched ten feet from side to side. The top of the desk was immaculate. Behind the desk, was a matching credenza, its top also clear. There were no pictures on any of the walls, nor were there any framed photos on either the desk or the credenza.

A man who appeared to be in his mid-to-late forties sat behind the desk. Longish brown hair, graying at the temples, gave him a handsome, distinguished look. He had a goatee, meticulously manicured, also brown and tinged with gray.

He wore a silk suit, tailor-made to fit his athletic frame. Must have cost more than a thousand dollars. Beneath his suit coat, he wore a powder blue dress shirt, the collar starched and sharp, a gold tie bar behind the knot of a royal blue silk tie. I couldn't tell if he was a lawyer or a banker or maybe the president of some major corporation. His appearance screamed that he was someone important, but a twinkle in his eye betrayed a sense of humor mixed with compassion. An important man; a powerful man; a kind man.

The door to the office opened and another man entered, also dressed in a silk suit—black—with a button-down shirt, also black. Black shoes polished to a high sheen. Black hair slicked back and held in place with hair gel. Black beard neatly trimmed. A black tie that was almost lost against the blackness of his shirt. A black carnation pinned to his lapel.

His eyes, too, showed importance and power, but had nary a trace of humor, kindness, or compassion. Not a kind man.

Neither of the two men seemed aware of my presence. When they spoke, it clanged memory bells for me. Where had I heard a conversation like that before? Of course. The night of the crash. Voices in my head.

"Hast thou considered my servant Job, that there is none like him in the earth, a perfect and upright man, one that feareth God and escheweth evil?"

"Doth Job fear God for naught? Take away your blessing, and he will curse thee to thy face."

But that's not what these voices were saying. It was a similar exchange, but not exactly the same. It was spoken in modern day English. A conversation that hit much closer to home.

The man behind the desk said, "I haven't seen you in a while. Where have you been?"

It was a cordial tone, but a wary one. Like opposing lawyers in a lawsuit talking to each other. Familiar opponents but feeling each other out on a new case. Professional, friendly, but each with his own agenda and his own client to protect.

"Oh, you know," the visitor said. "Here and there. Checking out your folks."

"I figured it was something like that. What do you think?"

"Like everything else, I guess. Some of 'em are good, some are bad. Some of them talk a good game, but you and I both know that talk's cheap. When it gets down to the lick-log, I'm not sure if you can really trust any of them."

The man at the desk rolled his chair back and stood. "Hold on a second and let me show you something."

He walked around his desk to the cabinets on his left. Found his way to a drawer labeled "F" and pulled it open. He thumbed his way past a number of files before settling on one. He pulled it out, closed the drawer, and returned to his desk but remained standing.

He opened the file and spun it around to face the visitor. There, clipped to the first page, was my picture. An older shot, taken for a press release when Juanita and I were first appointed to the mission field. I never really liked that picture. I thought it made me look too young and naïve, which I suppose I was at the time.

"Have you considered Corky Farris?" he asked the man in black. "He's one of a kind. There's no one else quite like him. He's a real jim-dandy, an upright man who fears God and shuns evil. What about him?"

The visitor approached the desk, leaned over, and looked at the file. A glimmer of recognition registered in his eyes.

"Yeah, I've seen him. I know who he is."

"Well, what do you think?"

The visitor picked up the folder and flipped through its pages. "Let's see, paratrooper in Japan, sings in church, school at Baylor and New Orleans. Pats puppy dogs on the head, I'm sure. He went to Japan, didn't he, as a missionary?"

"You know he did. It's right there in black and white. And I suspect you've seen him in action, especially in Japan. How many folks did he snatch right out of your claws?"

The visitor laughed. "Yeah, yeah, yeah. He did okay over there. But why isn't he still in Japan?"

"Because I was ready for him to go somewhere else. And he did what I wanted him to."

The visitor closed the folder and dropped it on the desk. Its edge hit the wood with an echoing *thunk.*

"And just why do you suspect he did what you wanted him to? Do you really think he serves you for nothing?"

"Not this old chestnut." The man behind the desk shook his head.

The visitor laughed again. "You know, maybe it's an old chestnut because there's so much truth to it. You've always protected ol'—what's his name again? Corky, is it? What kind of stupid name is that? Anyway, you've always protected ol' Corky and you've blessed his work. You've given him a good family. Loving wife and three loving kids. Of course he's happy now. Anyone would do what you wanted him to do as long as you bless him. But take away your blessing, and he'll curse you to your face. You'll see. I guarantee it."

"I think you're wrong."

"Wanna put your money where your mouth is?"

"What do you have in mind?"

"Let me throw a little adversity his way and let's see if he'll show a different color. I'm betting he will."

The man behind the desk thought about that for a minute. He picked up the file folder and flipped through its pages, then came to rest on the picture again. He studied it for a moment. Finally he said, "Okay, I'll tell you what. Do your worst to him with two caveats: leave his family alone and—"

"Nah, nah, I gotta be able to go after his family."

"You did once before, with Job. How'd that work out for you?"

The visitor remained silent.

"No, not this time," the office holder said. "Remember, you're testing him, not his wife and kids."

"Okay."

"The other caveat is that you have to spare his life."

"Now that's where I've got to draw the line. Spare his life? I don't know about that."

"It only makes logical sense. Same as with Job. How else will you know whether you've won? When he dies, he dies. But if you want to see whether he'll throw away his faith, well, doesn't he have to still be alive for you find out?"

The visitor in the black suit thought about it and then nodded. "Okay, I can work with that. I can do whatever I want to him though, right?"

"Right. But you don't get forever. We need to impose a time limit."

"What do you propose?"

"You're such a hot shot, you ought to be able to work quickly. I'll give you forty hours, not a second more."

"Forty hours, huh?"

"What, you don't think you can do it?"

"Oh, I can do it, all right."

"Then that's it. Forty hours or else no deal."

"Okay, deal."

There was no handshake to seal the deal. These two had obviously dealt with each other enough that their verbal agreement was all that was needed.

The office holder picked up the file and returned it to the filing cabinet. He looked over his shoulder as he closed the drawer to see that his visitor was still standing there, watching.

"What are you still doing here?" he said as he returned to his desk. "The clock's ticking."

With that, the visitor spun on his heels and left the office.

The office holder opened the bottom drawer, a deep drawer, on the right side of his desk and took out an hourglass. He turned it upside down and set it on the corner.

Sand began sliding down to the bottom half.

CHAPTER TWENTY-NINE

I still found myself engulfed in dark water, but I had a vague awareness of someone calling me, though not by my given name. I drifted upward and broke the surface of the water. I fought to clear the clouds that fogged my brain. It was a voice. A man's voice. A familiar voice. Gabe.

"Preacher," he said. "Hey, hey, preacher, wake up."

I still hurt, was still thirsty, was still cold. Just like I was before I had blacked out. No change. But that meant that I was still alive.

I squeezed my eyes even more tightly shut than they already were, then opened them. It took a moment for my vision to clear. As the images crystallized, I could see that Gabe stood over me, looking down into my face.

"Wake up sunshine," he said. "I was starting to think you'd left me."

"No, I'm still here. But I'm not sure if that's good or bad."

"It means you're still alive, so that's good."

"Besides," I said, "leaving is your trick."

"Which brings me to the bad news," he said. "I've got to go. For good this time."

"What does that mean, 'for good'?"

"Exactly what it sounds like. You won't see me again."

"Why?"

"I don't explain 'em, I just do 'em. But maybe, just maybe, it's because you don't need me anymore. I'm just guessing here, but let's go with it."

I wasn't sure what to make of that. Did this mean he really was a ghost, tied to some perimeter around his body and I had now reached the outskirts? Or was it because he had done all he could do as an angel and now he was leaving me on my own. Or had my brain finally recovered to the point that I was no longer hallucinating?

I looked back the way I had come. Even in the afternoon dimness of the forest floor, there was enough sunlight filtering through that I could make out the wreckage of the plane, maybe two football field lengths away, spotlighted by the rays. How could I possibly see that far in the denseness of the forest? I hadn't been able to see it before, so maybe I was still hallucinating, after all. I couldn't be sure.

"I need my jacket back," Gabe said.

"Why?"

"I just do."

"But it's cold. And you don't need it anymore."

"Yeah, I do. Don't know why; I just do."

I stared at him as if he was crazy, all the while wondering if I was the crazy one. Arguing with a dead man over the dead man's jacket. But it was his, after all.

I spied a fallen tree trunk close by, so I edged my way over to it, using my elbows. Then I inch-wormed my way into a semi-sitting position with my upper back and head resting against the trunk. I let loose my grip on the white dress shirt I had been dragging with me since waving it to get the attention of the illusionary children playing ring-around-the-rosie and leaned forward so I could take off the backpack and the flight jacket. Before I could even get one arm out of a sleeve, I saw that Gabe was already wearing it, standing in front of me.

I looked down at my torso. No flight jacket, just the black suit jacket I had worn when we took off from the airstrip outside Evadale. Had I ever really been wearing that flight jacket?

"Who am I going to talk to when you go?" I asked.

"Yourself." He laughed. "Or maybe you already have been."

Yeah, I had considered that. Gabe sure seemed real, though, ever since he first rose from the dead, so to speak. His probing questions and subtle—and some not so subtle—jabs were far more insightful than I was willing to give myself credit for. Up until we went down in the Big Thicket, I thought I had all the answers to the questions in my life, at least until that point. It almost seemed a betrayal of my faith to question God and His plan for my life the way Gabe had questioned it.

On the other hand, that process of analysis had led me to that one inescapable conclusion I reached before blacking out the last time: Every decision I made, right up to flying to Evadale a couple of days before, had been God's will for my life. And that provided an immeasurable comfort.

"I've just got one last thing to say to you before I go," Gabe said.

"I'm all ears."

"Wave your shirt."

"Huh?"

"Wave your shirt. Isn't that what you brought it for? So wave it."

And then he was gone. This time he didn't just fade off into the trees, but he simply vanished.

What strange last words. After all the things he'd said, all the questions he had raised, all the challenges he had leveled, was that really how he was going out? With "wave your shirt"? What did he mean by that?

I heard a man's voice in the near distance. Very faint and, at first, I couldn't make out where it was coming from, then I realized it was coming from the direction of the plane's wreckage. Gabe had obviously gone back to tether himself to his body and was calling some last bit of advice, or annoyance, to me. But when I looked toward the plane, I didn't see Gabe.

Instead, with my new version of super-vision, I saw a group of five men standing around the wrecked carcass of the plane. I had never seen any of them before. A sixth was kneeling next to Gabe's body, which was lying perpendicular to the fuselage.

I heard other voices, the group of men talking to each other, but their voices were indistinct.

A rescue party!

I gathered as much energy as I could and opened my mouth to yell, but nothing came out. I swallowed, tried to muster up some saliva in my mouth.

I opened it again. Another yell. This time my voice came out in a hoarse, throaty whisper, that decreased in volume the longer I yelled.

"Hey! Hey! Over here!"

Probably not audible that far away.

Then I thought of Gabe's last words: "Wave your shirt."

Of course. I gripped the white shirt by the tail and waved it over my head, twirling it around, the long sleeves flapping outward with each turn.

"Hey! Over here!" My voice was louder now.

One of the men turned and looked my way. I kept waving the shirt.

He appeared to say something to the others in an excited tone. They all turned and looked my way. I kept waving the shirt.

One of them pointed at me. Then, as a group, they began trotting toward me, picking their way over downed branches and a thick carpet of leaves.

Exhausted, I dropped my arm and rolled over onto my side. I wadded up the shirt and used it as a pillow while I waited. They had found me.

We had gone down Tuesday night at 10:30. Now, Thursday afternoon, they had found me.

On a whim I looked at my watch, which was still ticking: 2:30 p.m.

Forty hours.

EPILOGUE

From the Author

I was nine years old, in the fourth grade at Merrifield Elementary School in Duncanville, Texas, a southern suburb of Dallas, when my dad Dr. T.V. "Corky" Farris and pilot Len Rogers went down in the Big Thicket of southeast Texas on Tuesday night, January 12, 1965.

The fuselage of the green-and-white Mooney Mark 21 single engine aircraft came to rest on its belly on the floor of the forest, nose up against a tree. Len had suffered numerous internal injuries and, after he grew weaker over the first night, Pop decided to go for help Wednesday morning. In the near distance, he could hear sounds of traffic, so he headed in that direction. But the crash had broken his back (compression fractures; i.e., crushed vertebra), leaving him fully paralyzed from the waist down, so he had to resort to crawling by dragging his lower body with his elbows.

Thursday afternoon, Civil Air Patrol searchers spotted the wreckage, and a ground search team arrived at the site around 2:30, forty hours after the plane went down. One of the searchers noted two tall trees with gashes high on their trunks, indicating that the fuselage threaded the needle between them, which knocked the wings off simultaneously. Losing the wings, along with the attached gasoline tanks, accomplished two things: it prevented the plane from cartwheeling, and it was probably the only thing that kept the plane from catching fire.

The searchers found Pop a few hundred yards from the wreckage, where he had crawled until he blacked out and could go no farther. He didn't even know that Len had died until he was rescued. The highway with traffic he could hear was less than a mile from the site of the crash.

My mother Juanita had been holding down the fort during Pop's absence, trying to keep control of three kids until he got home. My sister Darlyne was eleven, in the sixth grade, and my brother Steve was four, in no grade. Because Len and Pop left from a tiny airstrip near Evadale, Texas, the night before they had originally planned to leave, without filing a flight plan, they had been down for anywhere between sixteen and eighteen hours before they were even missed by anyone, starting with Mom, who became concerned when Pop had not arrived home by Wednesday afternoon.

I'll always remember how I learned that Pop had been found. My fourth grade class had combined with the other fourth grade class in our school to watch a film. While it was playing, the principal spoke over the public address system and summoned my teacher, Ms. Walraven, to the office. She came back a few minutes later, approached me where I sat, and said in a very soft voice, "Mike, they found your daddy."

She then sent me to the office where my grandparents—my mother's mom and dad, whom we kids called Ma and Pa—waited. My mother had already left for Woodville, Texas, where Pop had been taken to a small hospital, and where he stayed for several weeks. He was then transferred to Baylor Hospital in Dallas for back surgery followed by months of physical rehabilitation. While he was in the hospital in Woodville and at Baylor, Mom stayed with him, while we three kids were farmed out to friends' homes.

I'll never forget the night when Pop was released from the hospital. His doctors had told him that he would never walk again but, though he had to wear a bulky metal-and-leather back brace, heavy leg braces, and arm-brace crutches, he walked out of the hospital and to the ambulance under his own power. When the ambulance arrived home, he also walked into our house under his own power. I still get teary-eyed thinking about it. Every kid who was ever threatened with "Just wait 'til your father gets home" should be so lucky. I was never happier for my father to get home. It had taken far too long.

I spent a lot of hours over the next year helping him with his exercises as he rehabbed at home. I'm not sure how much help I really was, at nine- and ten-years-old, but it was time I spent one-on-one with him that I'll always treasure. He ultimately was able to jettison the braces and walk using only a cane for balance.

That cane was both good and bad. Good, because he was able to walk. Bad, because it gave him something to wave in the air at school performances and football games to embarrass us in front of our friends. At an 8th grade choir performance while I was in junior high, I was one of four boys designated by the director to perform a pitiful soft-shoe while the choir sang "East Side, West Side." Actually, she didn't assign us to perform a pitiful soft-shoe, just a soft-shoe; we improvised the pitiful part on our own. Even with the lights in my eyes on stage, I could see that cane swirling in the air at the back of the school auditorium.

In March of 1970, Pop left the Evangelism Division and accepted the pastorate of Gaston Avenue Baptist Church in Dallas, which necessitated our move from Duncanville to the Lakewood area of east Dallas and brought me to Woodrow Wilson High School for the start of my sophomore year. While Pop was at Gaston Avenue, he had some problems with a few of the church leaders (who, I might add, had already run off his predecessor), though I was unaware of it at the time, and which culminated in his resignation as pastor in the spring of 1972. Award-winning religion reporter Helen Parmley reported it like this in *The Dallas Morning News*:

> The pastor and director of music at the Gaston Avenue Baptist Church unexpectedly submitted their resignations to a stunned group of worshipers attending the services at the church Sunday night. Dr. Theorn [sic] V. Farris, in an

> emotion-packed statement, *The Dallas News*
> learned, said he found objections to his ministry
> 'intolerable' and was therefore submitting his
> resignation, effective April 2. Dr. and Mrs. Farris
> then left the meeting followed by Tom Bledsoe,
> minister of music, who said his resignation was
> effective immediately.

Ms. Parmley wrote that "If the resignations stand, the 4,500 member church's staff will consist of one part-time minister of youth, since the minister of education resigned two months ago." She used the word "if" because the church membership voted to reject the resignation.

Among the "objections" that Pop found intolerable were criticisms that "encouraged him to minimize his evangelistic preaching" and that "questioned the emotional aspects of his preaching," as well as objecting to my mother working (at the Baptist Building in Dallas where she was a secretary in the Evangelism Division), which supposedly kept her from carrying out her "duties" as the pastor's wife. The critics also questioned whether he could "effectively carry out his ministry with his 'handicap'" – a reference to that walking with a cane business I mentioned above; you know, from the plane crash that broke his back after he led an evangelistic meeting in east Texas.

Sticking with his resignation despite the congregation's vote to reject it, Pop took a position as professor of Hebrew and Old Testament at Mid-America Baptist Theological Seminary, which had just opened in Little Rock, Arkansas. The founder of the seminary, Dr. B. Gray Allison, had been one of his professors at New Orleans Baptist Theological Seminary. It was he who had introduced Pop to Dr. John Abernathy, who had participated in the Shantung Revival in China. Dr. Allison was also on the thesis committee that awarded Pop his doctorate.

I heard a story Mom told about the thesis committee having no questions for Pop when he presented the oral defense of his thesis, "Degrees of Definiteness in the Aramaic Genitive Relationships in the Book of Daniel," a story Dr. Allison later confirmed. He explained that they had no questions because it was clear that Pop knew more than they did on the subject.

Darlyne had already graduated from high school by then, but the plan was that our family would remain in Dallas, so that Steve and I wouldn't have to change schools, while Pop commuted to Little Rock during the weeks and home on weekends. But then the unexpected happened. A group of members from Gaston Avenue split off to form a new church, and then called Pop to be their first pastor.

He agreed, though only on a part-time basis since he had already committed to the new seminary in Little Rock. Over the course of the next semester, he commuted between jobs, living in Little Rock during the week and returning to Dallas on weekends to serve as the first pastor of the newly-formed Forest Meadow Baptist Church. At the end of the school year, he resigned from the seminary to remain in Dallas as full-time pastor at Forest Meadow.

At its inception, Forest Meadow was almost like a floating card game, meeting for a time in the basement of Ross Avenue State Bank in east Dallas and then sharing space with Saint Stephen United Methodist Church in Mesquite, before later holding services in the band hall at Forest Meadow Junior High School in north Dallas. After a couple of years, it finally built a building of its own.

While at Forest Meadow, Pop continued a pattern he had started at Gaston Avenue of using music and drama as part of his sermons, which was way ahead of its time in the early 1970s, and most likely an outgrowth of his initial interest in entering into the music ministry. He also he structured a Creative Preaching workshop for local Dallas pastors, and he wrote or co-

217 / **Forty Hours**

wrote two full-length dramas, which were performed multiple times at churches in Dallas. One of those dramas, called "Doomstar," was about the Second Coming of Christ. The other, called "The Golgotha Affair," was inspired by the Watergate hearings and depicted an investigation by the Roman Senate into the circumstances surrounding, and leading up to, the crucifixion of Jesus.

After a few years, Pop left Forest Meadow and returned to Mid-America Seminary, which by then had relocated to Memphis, TN. He spent the last seventeen years of his life there as chairman of the Old Testament and Hebrew Department, teaching courses not only in Hebrew and Old Testament, but also creating and teaching a course in creative preaching. During that time, he co-wrote, co-produced, and starred in two half-hour television specials that aired locally. One told the story of Job, from the Old Testament, while the other told the story of Naaman, the Syrian commander in the Old Testament who was afflicted with leprosy.

It was also while he was at Mid-America that my mother died of breast cancer, which left a hole in his heart. It culminated a roughly 18-month span in which he lost not only his wife, but also his mother and his sole surviving brother, his other brother and his father having passed away years earlier.

Although he later remarried, I believe that Juanita always remained his first love. I heard him once recount his struggles during the time she suffered with her malignancy, and how his prayers underwent a transformation. They started as prayers for her healing, then changed to prayers simply that her pain be eased. He talked of a willingness to die instead of his loved one, then a willingness to die with his loved one. Finally, he placed the whole matter in God's hands and told the Lord that whatever happened was okay with him. God then gave him peace.

That was why, when God took her home, he could write: "It is at this point that the message of the Gospel and the hope of eternity take on a new and sweeter meaning. To be perfectly honest, I seem to have more investment on the other side than here. Won't it be a glorious day when we can be reunited with those we love?"

Pop was still teaching at Mid-America when he, himself, passed away on December 14, 1993, shortly after publication of his book *Mighty to Save: A Study in Old Testament Soteriology* (soteriology is defined as the doctrine of salvation). On his last visit to Texas in July of 1993, he gave a copy of the book to my wife and me with the inscription: "To Mike and Susan, As a token of my love – and something to remember me by. As ever, Daddy (Pop) 7/1/93"

It was almost as if he knew his days were numbered.

The question arises as to whether he ever fulfilled that sense of divine appointment he talked about following his missionary service in Japan and the plane crash. I believe he did. I believe that sense of divine appointment was not for a single event, such as a Shantung Revival, but rather it was for a lifetime of ministry and service.

Pop continued his ministry even after the crash, as an evangelist, pastor, and then seminary professor, and also as a friend. I'll never forget talking to the steady stream of visitors at his funeral, many of whom I had never met before. Each one had a story to tell, separate and distinct. Something funny, something poignant, something inspiring. Each story brought a smile or a tear or a laugh, or perhaps all three. But a common theme ran through them all. He had touched lives. He had comforted, cheered, ministered, counseled, and witnessed. He had cared and he had loved. And everybody he touched loved him back.

What better appointment can there be?

Pop always believed that the experience of those forty hours in The Big Thicket and being tied to a cane for the rest of his life, painful and inconvenient though they were, gave him credibility to minister to others who had suffered pain and loss. Clearly, God spared his life for a reason.

Here's how he summed up the experience:

"Some people have said, off and on across the years, 'When you get to heaven, the Lord will explain to you why you had to carry that cane.' And my response has been, 'Well, He may. But we have an agreement: So far as I'm concerned, He's under no obligation to mention it.' But I have a feeling that, if He should say, 'Hey, Farris, let me explain to you why you had to carry that cane all those years,' surely my response will be, 'Lord, what cane was that?'"

Other books by Mike Farris

NOVELS

Miles Apart
Something Unfortunate
The Catch
Every Pig Got a Saturday
Isle of Broken Dreams
Wrongful Termination
The Bequest
Rules of Privilege
Manifest Intent
Kanaka Blues

NON-FICTION

Poor Innocent Lad: The Tragic Death of Gill Jamieson and the
Execution of Myles Fukunaga
Fifty Shades of Black & White: Anatomy of the Lawsuit Behind a
Publishing Phenomenon
A Death in the Islands: The Unwritten Law and the Last Trial of
Clarence Darrow
Call Me Lucky: A Texan in Hollywood

Readers can contact Mike at msfarris1@att.net, and can find
him on Facebook. (1) Mike Farris | Facebook

www.ingramcontent.com/pod-product-compliance
Lightning Source LLC
Chambersburg PA
CBHW051508260626
47162CB00008B/2870

* 9 7 8 1 9 5 0 2 9 2 0 8 0 *